Dear Reader,

We're thrilled that some of Harlequin's most famous families are making an encore appearance! With this special Famous Families fifty-book collection, we are proud to offer you the chance to relive the drama, the glamour, the suspense and the romance of four of Harlequin's most beloved families—the Fortunes, the Bravos, the McCabes and the Cavanaughs.

Our third family, the McCabes, welcomes you to Laramie, Texas. A small ranching town of brick buildings, awnings and shady streets, Laramie is the kind of place where everyone knows each other. The little town is currently abuzz with wedding plans—and no McCabe is safe from the matchmaking! The path to the altar may not be smooth for the McCabes, but their humor-filled journeys will no doubt bring a smile to your face.

And in August, you'll be captivated by our final family, the Cavanaughs. Generations of Cavanaughs have protected the citizens of Aurora, California. But can they protect themselves from falling in love? You won't want to miss any of these stories from *USA TODAY* bestselling author Marie Ferrarella!

Happy reading,

The Editors

CATHY GILLEN THACKER

is married and a mother of three. She and her husband spent eighteen years in Texas and now reside in North Carolina. Her mysteries, romance comedies and heartwarming family stories have made numerous appearances on bestseller lists, but her best reward, she says, is knowing that one of her books made someone's day a little brighter. A popular Harlequin Books author for many years, she loves telling passionate stories with happy endings, and thinks nothing beats a good romance and a hot cup of tea! You can visit Cathy's website, www.cathygillenthacker.com, for more information on her upcoming and previously published books, recipes and a list of her favorite things.

FAMOUS FAMILIES

the McCABES

CATHY GILLEN THACKER

The Last Virgin in Texas

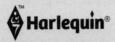

Harlequin®

TORONTO NEW YORK LONDON
AMSTERDAM PARIS SYDNEY HAMBURG
STOCKHOLM ATHENS TOKYO MILAN MADRID
PRAGUE WARSAW BUDAPEST AUCKLAND

Recycling programs
for this product may
not exist in your area.

ISBN-13: 978-0-373-36511-1

THE LAST VIRGIN IN TEXAS

Copyright © 2012 by Cathy Gillen Thacker

Originally published as THE VIRGIN BRIDE SAID, "WOW!"

Copyright © 2001 by Cathy Gillen Thacker

This edition published by arrangement with Harlequin Books S.A.

For questions and comments about the quality of this book please contact us at Customer_eCare@Harlequin.ca.

® and TM are trademarks of the publisher. Trademarks indicated with ® are registered in the United States Patent and Trademark Office, the Canadian Trade Marks Office and in other countries.

www.Harlequin.com

Printed in U.S.A.

FAMOUS FAMILIES

The Fortunes

Cowboy at Midnight by Ann Major
A Baby Changes Everything by Marie Ferrarella
In the Arms of the Law by Peggy Moreland
Lone Star Rancher by Laurie Paige
The Good Doctor by Karen Rose Smith
The Debutante by Elizabeth Bevarly
Keeping Her Safe by Myrna Mackenzie
The Law of Attraction by Kristi Gold
Once a Rebel by Sheri WhiteFeather
Military Man by Marie Ferrarella
Fortune's Legacy by Maureen Child
The Reckoning by Christie Ridgway

The Bravos by Christine Rimmer

The Nine-Month Marriage
Marriage by Necessity
Practically Married
Married by Accident
The Millionaire She Married
The M.D. She Had to Marry
The Marriage Agreement
The Bravo Billionaire
The Marriage Conspiracy
His Executive Sweetheart
Mercury Rising
Scrooge and the Single Girl

The McCabes by Cathy Gillen Thacker

Dr. Cowboy
Wildcat Cowboy
A Cowboy's Woman
A Cowboy Kind of Daddy
A Night Worth Remembering
The Seven-Year Proposal
The Dad Next Door
The Last Virgin in Texas
Texas Vows: A McCabe Family Saga
The Ultimate Texas Bachelor
Santa's Texas Lullaby
A Texas Wedding Vow
Blame It on Texas
A Laramie, Texas Christmas
From Texas, With Love

The Cavanaughs by Marie Ferrarella

Racing Against Time
Crime and Passion
Internal Affair
Dangerous Games
The Strong Silent Type
Cavanaugh's Woman
In Broad Daylight
Alone in the Dark
Dangerous Disguise
The Woman Who Wasn't There
Cavanaugh Watch
Cavanaugh Heat

Chapter 1

"They turned us down again, didn't they?" Brady Anderson guessed, as Kelsey Lockhart strode across the sunny pasture toward him, her cheeks pink with temper, her tousled hair glowing as cinnamon-red as the leaves in the maple trees around them.

Kelsey's long slender legs continued eating up the ground until she reached his side. Tipping her flat-brimmed hat back off her forehead, she met his searching gaze and reported unhappily, "Yep, they sure did. That's the fifteenth bank that's said no to us because we didn't have enough collateral."

Brady grinned, trying, as always, when he was this close to her, not to notice how very pretty Kelsey was in an outdoorsy, lady rancher sort of way. Personally, he'd never been much for redheads. They were a bit too temperamental for his taste. And Kelsey Lockhart, the youngest of the four delectable Lockhart sisters of Laramie, Texas, was that, for sure. But there was something about the pale gold freckles dotting her smooth golden skin, the lusciousness of her full lips that had his gaze returning to her face again and again. Chuckling, he looked into her dark green eyes, which were now flashing with both frustration and impatience, as he commiserated humorously, "You'd think we'd get the hint, wouldn't you?"

Kelsey leaned against the part of the aging wooden fence he hadn't yet treated with wood preservative. Unlike him, she refused to take this latest rejection in stride. She folded her arms in front of her contentiously and glared at him, wanting answers. Now. This instant. "What are we going to do?" Her expressive red brows slammed down over her long-lashed eyes. "We can't buy the rest of the horses and cattle unless we get a loan. And since no bank will give it to us, and we haven't had the resources to make a killing in the stock market again…" Kelsey's voice trailed off in discouragement.

Brady shared Kelsey's frustration about that, since it was a talent for investing that had drawn them together initially and enabled them both to come up with the cash for the down payment on their ranch the previous summer. If they had another six months and enough seed money to get started, maybe they could do it again. Maybe. But they didn't have either the time or the seed money. Which left them fewer options. Brady put down his brush and wiped his hands with the cloth he had looped into his belt. The rest of the painting would have to wait. "Then we look for a venture capitalist to underwrite the rest of our setup expenses," Brady said, having already anticipated just such a move being necessary. He put the lid back on the bucket of wood preservative, picked up his brush and gave Kelsey a confidence-inspiring look. "And I know just the one."

An hour later, Kelsey and Brady were sitting in Wade McCabe's office on the Golden Slipper Ranch that he shared with his wife, Josie.

A stellar businessman himself, Wade listened patiently to their plans for expanding Kelsey's horse-riding stables and Brady's cattle operation, and reviewed their business plans, which Brady knew full well were solid as a rock. And then Wade zeroed in on the same thing all the bankers had. "Unfortunately, the two of you aren't married," Wade said, with a disapproving frown.

"So?" Kelsey said, spoiling for a fight about that—one of many they'd had with literally everyone who had learned how they'd impulsively pooled their resources so they could make their individual dreams of owning their own ranch come true, sooner rather than later.

"That's true," Brady interrupted coolly, putting up a hand before Kelsey could go all contentious and argumentative on them. He looked Wade straight in the eye. "But we did buy back the ranch that belonged to her folks. We've been in partnership for four months now. That ought to count for something." Especially since most people in Laramie hadn't thought he and Kelsey would last more than a few weeks together, at most.

Wade sighed and handed back their business plan. "Look, Brady, I know you're a good man and a talented cowboy—otherwise my brother Travis wouldn't have hired you to work on his ranch—but that doesn't mean I approve of what you're doing with Kelsey here."

Brady had an idea what Wade was hinting at— that he was somehow taking advantage of the six-year age difference and Kelsey's youth to get what he wanted. "We're business partners, Wade," Brady told him. "Pure and simple."

Wade nodded. "Yeah, I heard you've been sleeping in the tack room in the stables since you moved out to the ranch, and have even rigged up a little bathroom and outdoor shower for yourself there."

"Nothing untoward has gone on between us," Kelsey interrupted, beginning to look very ticked off that anyone could even suspect there had been. "Not that it would be any business of yours or anyone else's if there had been!" she finished angrily.

Wade lifted a brow in a way that said "The lady doth protest too much."

Brady knew how Wade felt. If he didn't know better, he'd think by Kelsey's defensive reaction and the blush in her cheeks that there *was* something going on between them. Not that it would have been surprising if there had been, from a strictly physical perspective. Kelsey was one very sexy woman. She was half a foot shorter than Brady, with a slender, athletic body that curved in all the right places. Very much a tomboy. Notoriously fickle. But somehow very innocent, nevertheless. She had a way about her that somehow made her everybody's kid sister. And yet there was nothing siblinglike about the increasingly lustful feelings he was beginning to have for her, Brady knew.

Was that what Wade McCabe was picking up

on? Was that what had Wade, and everyone else who knew them, concerned about the partnership between him and the black sheep of the Lock-hart family? Brady wondered, his glance taking in Kelsey's snug-fitting jeans and red cowgirl boots. The man's denim work shirt she wore knotted at her hips was loose enough to conceal the abundant curves of her breasts and her slender waist—the figure-hugging tank top she wore beneath was not.

"Kelsey," Brady finally said, before Kelsey could make the two of them look even guiltier with her hot-tempered protests, "Wade is not in-terested in our love life or lack thereof. Not that there is one, you understand," Brady finished firmly, looking at Wade. Regardless of how much he desired Kelsey, he had never once so much as tried to kiss her. For one thing, he didn't want to be another notch on Kelsey's belt. He figured to date and then be dumped by her, as she appar-ently dumped every man sooner or later, would be the kiss of death for their partnership. Because he doubted he could ever get over that. For another, he didn't think he should get involved with her when he still had some very sticky problems of his own to deal with—a secret debt of his own that was coming due in two weeks. A debt that could change the way she felt about him, permanently, once she realized all he had been keeping from her and everyone else in Laramie. She might understand him not telling everyone about the rash promises he had made and the debt he owed. A debt he still had no way to effectively settle, without a loan from a venture capitalist like Wade McCabe. But she wouldn't understand him not telling her. Not when his earlier actions could leave her partnerless in another two weeks.

"That's good to hear," Wade continued with a warning look at Brady, picking up their conversation where Brady had left off, "because Kelsey is like a kid sister to me and I wouldn't want to think you or anyone else had taken advantage of her."

"Wade, could you please just forget about my personal life and concentrate on business. I'm trying to get a loan from you here—not advice to the *not* necessarily lovelorn."

Brady grinned at her cute play on words.

Wade was amused, but he didn't grin. "Kelsey, I am a businessman, pure and simple," he told her firmly, standing to signal the meeting was over. "I don't make bad investments. If I had I never would have been a millionaire by the time I was thirty. And the bottom line is, this partnership of yours and Brady's does not look like something that is going to stand the test of time to me."

"Thanks, anyway." Brady stood, too, and held out his hand, to let Wade know there were no hard feelings. Maybe the trick here was to go to a venture capitalist who didn't know them personally. Someone who didn't feel so protective of Kelsey.

Ignoring Brady's hint that they cut the meeting short and make a dignified exit, Kelsey glared at Brady, who was still shaking hands with Wade McCabe. She slipped her hands in the pockets of her jeans. "Oh, really, and how do you figure that, Wade?" She lifted her chin, the look she gave Wade as contentious as the rising tenor of her voice. "Do you have some sort of businessman's crystal ball?"

"No," Wade returned evenly, abruptly looking as if he were an exasperated father talking to a wayward child. He clamped his lips together. "But I do know your history with men and jobs, Kelsey."

Oh, man, Brady thought, having heard this same spiel or something like it from everyone in Laramie County.

"And you never stay with either very long," Wade continued flatly, not about to back down from his stance any more than Kelsey was. "The bottom line? The only way I'd loan you and Brady money is if you were married."

"Well, that's it then," Kelsey said as she and Brady walked back out to the Lockhart-Anderson

Ranch pickup truck. She thrust out her chin defiantly. "We'll just get married. Today."

Brady rolled his eyes. "Kelse, be serious."

"I am." She stomped closer. "We need the money to expand. You need more cattle, fence and feed to start turning a profit on your side of the ranch. And I need more horses, another stable to house them, and the money to hire some instructors so I can teach all those kids and adults who want riding lessons from me. The only way that will happen is if we get a loan."

"I agree we need more money as soon as possible," Brady said. He opened the passenger door for Kelsey.

Instead of getting in, she leaned against the side of the truck. "Then let's get hitched and get it," she suggested in her usual carefree manner.

Brady frowned. As much as he hated to admit it, he could see himself married to Kelsey. He could also see them in bed. Making love. And doing any number of things that would lead to nothing but trouble. He had just sworn to Wade McCabe he would keep Kelsey out of trouble. Not lead her into it. "Marriage is serious business, Kelse," he reminded her sternly.

A mixture of curiosity and devilry sparkled in her dark green eyes. "You say that as if you know," Kelsey taunted.

Brady hated being the responsible one in any relationship. But when he was with Kelsey, that was exactly what role he usually found himself playing. "Well, I do," he retorted evenly.

Kelsey's lips parted slightly in an "oh" of surprise as she continued to study him carefully. "Have you ever been married?"

"No." Deliberately, Brady pushed aside the memory of his near-miss. "You?"

"No," Kelsey replied rapidly, the look she gave him letting him know she had never been anywhere close. Which wasn't a surprise, given her notoriously fickle history with men. "But that doesn't mean I couldn't be if it were necessary for business reasons," Kelsey continued. "And let's face it, it is." She stood, legs braced, heels dug into the gravel driveway beneath her feet. "The only way anyone, whether it be bank or venture capitalist, is going to give us any money is if we first demonstrate enough stability to prove to them it will be a sound investment, either by cohabiting on our ranch for a very long time, like a matter of years, or going the traditional route and already being happily married. Besides—" she shrugged "—it will get everyone who thinks I shouldn't be partnering with you, because it will prevent my ever falling in love and/or getting married to anyone else, off my back."

She had a point there, Brady admitted reluctantly to himself. He braced a hand on the roof of the pickup, next to her head. "I thought the wedding fever that had swept town last summer had sort of died down," he countered, looking down at her.

"Hah!" New color swept Kelsey's cheeks, making the golden splattering of freckles across her cheeks and nose stand out all the more. "It's only gotten worse since Sam McCabe and Kate Marten got married last week. John and Lilah McCabe are dropping hints about me marching down the aisle." She looked at Brady, her frustration as evident as her determination to do something about it, something reckless, something they wouldn't want her to do. "My sisters make no secret about how much they want me to marry," she continued hotly.

"But you've told everyone under the sun you are never getting married, ever, no matter what." As far as Brady was concerned, that should settle it. But it didn't. Not for the Lockhart sisters, the McCabes, or even, it seemed, Kelsey herself, who had seemed to get more and more antsy about the subject as time went by, Brady noted.

Kelsey bent her knee and propped the sole of one boot against the side of the pickup. "So?" she shot back mischievously. "I'm notoriously fickle, remember? I change my mind all the time. I've had several dozen different jobs in the past six years, and many, many more boyfriends. This will be just another indication of my flightiness."

Brady regarded her in exasperation. He couldn't deny being involved with Kelsey—even as merely business partners—brought an endless array of surprises. But there was a limit as to what he was willing to do, even to achieve his dreams of being a successful rancher and self-made man. With a great deal more patience than he felt, he explained, "Kelse, we can't just say 'I do' and then move in together and live under the same roof and have everything magically work out."

Kelsey looked shocked. Abruptly, she moved away from him. "Who said anything about living under the same roof?" she spouted, looking abruptly as irritated with him as he was with her. She poked a finger against his chest. "I'm talking about a marriage of convenience here, a business arrangement, Brady. I just want to get hitched long enough to get our money."

Brady released his breath in a whoosh of frustration. "Doing something purely for the sake of money is always a bad thing, Kelse." He knew, having already done so himself. In fact, it was the agreement he'd made two years ago that was likely to be the end of life as he wanted it, yet.

"But building up our business isn't." Kelsey

turned pleading eyes to his. She grabbed both his hands and squeezed them in hers. "Please, Brady." She looked up at him in a way he was hard-pressed to deny. "Let's get hitched. Now. Today."

"You did what?" Wade McCabe asked two hours later.

"We got married at city hall," Kelsey announced, still carrying the bouquet of Texas wildflowers Brady'd gotten her before they'd gone into the courthouse.

"This isn't funny," Wade said, after studying the marriage certificate they'd handed him, for proof. Wade glared at Brady.

"Believe me, it's no joke to us, either," Brady replied. He was pretty sure it was the overbearing, intensely protective nature of all those around her that had pushed Kelsey to be the wildly reckless woman she was.

"So let's talk money," Kelsey said, grabbing Brady's hand and plopping herself down in a chair in front of Wade's desk. "Brady and I were thinking prime plus one, in terms of interest rates."

"Payable in six months, max," Brady added firmly, as he took the chair next to Kelsey's. He didn't want them beholden to Wade any longer than possible.

"There's no way you can do that," Wade argued.

Actually, Brady thought silently, there was. Although even Kelsey didn't know about the way he was going to do that....

"By then, we figure we'll have established enough of a history and a business to be able to get another loan, from either a venture capitalist or a bank," Kelsey said seriously, looking and acting like the top-notch businesswoman she was.

"Okay. I'll give you the money you want," Wade said, "but I've got some conditions, too."

Although he wasn't anxious to learn what they were, Brady had expected as much.

"Such as...?" Kelsey prodded.

"If this marriage of yours proves to be a fraud, I get the deed to your ranch, free and clear." Wade gave that a moment to sink in, then continued, even more seriously, "It's not too late to back out. Because unless I miss my guess," Wade continued, looking from one of them to the other, "this is still at the stage where it can all quietly be undone, maybe without even an annulment if you're lucky enough. People will know what happened, of course—since you went to city hall—but the mistake won't be a permanent or long-lasting kind of thing, and you'll still have your ranch."

"Just not the loan money from you," Brady guessed quietly.

Wade nodded. He looked at Brady as if he

thought Brady should have known better than to get sucked into one of Kelsey's wild ideas. Unfortunately, Brady knew that was true.

"Fine. Draw up the papers," Kelsey said heatedly.

"I mean it, Kelsey." Wade frowned all the more. "If you insist on doing this…on trying to pull something over on me and everyone else, I'll take your ranch," Wade warned.

Brady had only to look at Wade to believe him. This was the only way Wade thought he could protect Kelsey from herself. Not surprisingly, Kelsey kept her hold on Brady's hand. "I married this man. I'm staying married to him," she announced boldly. "Now, draw up the papers, Wade. 'Cause as soon as you do, we're signing on the dotted line."

Kelsey and Brady went straight to the bank, then headed back to the ranch. They were still wearing the boots, jeans, denim work shirts and hats they'd had on earlier in the day. The only difference were the matching dime-store wedding rings on their left ring fingers. "See," Kelsey said after a while, trying not to worry about what she'd recklessly insisted they get themselves into, "I told you it'd be fine."

Brady's black brows drew together. To Kelsey's

consternation, he didn't exactly look as if he agreed with her.

"Absolutely nothing has changed," Kelsey continued, as she studied Brady's strong, six-foot frame. Although he tended to be a little mysterious—he never talked to anyone about the life he'd had before he had landed in Laramie, Texas—there wasn't a finer-looking cowboy or more capable cattleman around, as far as she was concerned. He was solidly muscled from head to toe and had shoulders that were broad enough to lean on. Not that she'd ever really done so. A suntanned face, and a smile that was sexy and reckless enough to make her heart skip a beat. And he made a good partner, too.

Brady turned his pickup truck into the lane, the fading afternoon sunlight casting shadows along their path. "Well, I wouldn't say that, exactly," he said, nodding at the proliferation of cars and trucks in their drive. As she turned her gaze in the direction of his, it was all Kelsey could do not to groan out loud. It looked like a convention of the Lockharts and the McCabes. He turned to Kelsey expectantly. "Are we having a party I didn't know about?" he asked.

Kelsey frowned, then allowed hesitantly, "Maybe a wedding reception."

Brady's lips came together firmly. He slanted her a glance. "What?"

"Well, you know my sisters." Kelsey shrugged off the concern in Brady's midnight-blue eyes. "And now that the word is out, they probably want to throw us a party or something to welcome you to the family." As well as chew her out, big-time, for not inviting them to witness the ceremony when they were all right there in town and could easily have attended and or tried to talk her out of doing such a reckless and impulsive thing in the first place.

Brady cut the motor on the pickup. "Sounds like fun," he said unenthusiastically.

Judging by the surly look on his face, Kelsey guessed, the duplicity of what they had done was beginning to get to Brady, too. But knowing there was no going back and undoing anything, especially now that they had the money they needed sitting in the bank, Kelsey pushed open her door and jumped down from the truck. "I just hope they don't have our family minister in there," Kelsey said. If she had to say her vows in front of clergy, she'd really feel married. And she didn't want to feel linked to Brady in that way. It was going to be hard enough as it was, pretending to one and all they were truly head over heels in love when they were in public. Noting Brady looked as alarmed about that prospect as she was feeling, Kelsey quickly reassured him. "They probably just have a cake or a wedding dress from my sister Jenna's shop that they want me to wear for pictures. I'm sure we won't have to say our vows again." It had been hard enough rushing through the words the first time, without really meaning or even concentrating on the promises they were making to each other.

"Good." Brady released a short sigh of relief. He lifted his hat and ran his hand through the inky-black layers of his hair, straightening the tousled layers as best he could. "'Cause, uh…"

"I understand perfectly," Kelsey said, cutting him off and letting him know with a quick, decisive look that it wasn't necessary to say more, as he slammed his hat back on his head and circled around the truck to join her. She knew he didn't want to have to fib to people about the nature of their relationship any more than she did. "And I quite agree." She linked hands with him— as much for moral support as show—and drew a deep breath, still holding her bouquet of Texas wildflowers and their certificate of marriage close to her chest. "There's only so much pretending a body can take in one day." Drawing strength from both his touch and the look in his eyes, she said, "Ready to go in and face the music?"

"Sure." Brady grinned, abruptly looking as determined and devil-may-care as Kelsey had felt earlier. He shrugged and tightened his hand on hers. "Why not?"

Chapter 2

"I can't believe you did this," Meg Lockhart said the moment Kelsey and Brady walked in the door.

"So much for any hopes of a wedding reception," Kelsey said lightly, as she looked at the faces gathered around her. Her oldest sister, Meg, was there with her doctor-husband Luke Carrigan. Second-oldest Jenna stood next to her, looking fashionably pretty in one of her own designs, with her rancher-businessman husband, Jake. Dani, who was closest in age to Kelsey and could usually be counted on to understand her little sister, was seated on the sofa, with her movie-star husband, Beau Chamberlain. Lilah and John McCabe rounded out the party. All looked grim, worried and very, very concerned about the nuptials that had just taken place, sans festivities of any kind. "This feels like an intervention," Kelsey continued joking, hoping to bring a little levity to the situation.

"It is," Jenna said. "And I called it."

"Thanks, heaps." Kelsey took off her hat and hung it on the rack next to the front door. She strode across the polished wood floor. "Just what Brady and I needed on our wedding night, a lecture times eight."

"Believe it or not," Dani said as she stood and put her right hand on her rounded tummy, "we just have your best interests at heart."

"We're all worried about you," Meg agreed gently but firmly.

"Well, you needn't be," Kelsey shot right back. She linked her arm through Brady's and put her head on his shoulder. "Because Brady and I are happy as can be."

Everyone in the room sighed and frowned at that.

"You know we promised your parents we'd watch over you girls," Lilah McCabe said.

"I'm not sure a business arrangement called a marriage is what they would want for you, Kelsey," John McCabe added.

Kelsey's conscience ignited like a match to a flame. Stubbornly, she pushed any doubts she had about what she was doing aside. In this case, she told herself firmly, the end did justify the means. "On the contrary, Dr. McCabe, I think they'd be very happy to see the ranch back in the family, and looking so good again."

"I don't think that's what John and Lilah mean," Jenna said a little testily.

Kelsey glared at her sister.

"We want you to have love, Kelsey," Meg added.

"Passion," Dani agreed.

"Not to mention a relationship that will stand the test of time," John elaborated bluntly. He looked at Brady.

"Well, thank you all for your vote of confidence," Kelsey said, more irritated than ever at the depth of familial interference going on. "But Brady and I want to be alone now, so…if you don't mind…"

"Kelsey—" Meg started.

Knowing there was only one way to end it as quickly as she wanted to end it, Kelsey turned to her new husband, grabbed him by the shirtfront and tugged him toward her. She barely had time to register the surprise in his eyes before she planted a big kiss right on his lips.

* * *

Brady heard the gasps around him as Kelsey's soft, luscious lips pressed against his. He had two choices. He could push her away, which would humiliate her even more than she already had been that day by her own actions and the words of others. Or he could play along. Given how good, how right her lips felt molded to his, Brady decided to play along. Not content to be a passive participant at anything he did, he wrapped his arms around her waist and pulled her up on tiptoe, so she was pressed even closer to him. And then the world faded away, as it became just the two of them. Locked together.

Only the sound of a collective "ahem" brought them back to reality. Reluctantly, Brady lifted his lips from hers and looked down at Kelsey. Her lips were dewy and pink, her eyes dazed with the same kind of wonder he felt. Heck of a first kiss, he thought. *Heck of a first kiss.*

"You know, maybe there's a little more going on here than we realized." Lilah McCabe was the first to speak.

"I think we should go and leave the newlyweds alone," John McCabe concurred. He and Lilah led the way out the door, followed by the Lockhart sisters and their husbands.

"You hurt her," Jake said to Brady, "you deal

with us." Beau and Luke nodded their confirmation of that threat. "You call if you need anything," Beau told Kelsey sympathetically, before he exited with the group.

Jenna came back in. She put a key on the table beside the door. "My apartment above the shop is empty right now. Should either of you need it, for any reason, you feel free to use it." She left again, too.

Motors started up. One by one, the vehicles headed down the lane to the highway. Kelsey looked at Brady. Brady looked at Kelsey. She had never looked more beautiful or desirable to him than she did at that very moment. He sighed. This was going to be a lot harder than he'd thought. A lot harder. Given the way she had just felt in his arms, he didn't know how in the heck he was going to keep their relationship platonic. "I hate to say it, Kelse," he drawled, "but I think we've just gotten ourselves into one heck of a mess."

Kelsey couldn't help but notice the mixture of derision and regret in Brady's low tone. Suddenly, it seemed the Lockharts and the McCabes weren't the only ones worried about what she and Brady had done. Determined not to let herself fall prey to the same pessimism, Kelsey propped her hands on her hips and lifted her chin. "Why in the world would you say that?"

Brady rolled his eyes and continued to pace. "Besides the fact I've got the whole Lockhart-McCabe 'army' breathing down my neck?"

"They're a little excited." Kelsey plopped down on the sofa as if she hadn't a care in the world. She shrugged, and continued, "They'll get over it."

Brady's lips curved up on either side. "Before or after they pulverize me?" he asked. His probing glance made a leisurely tour of her body before returning to her eyes. "And speaking of pulverizing me, what was that kiss about just now?"

Kelsey had hoped he would be too nice a partner to bring that up. Guess not. Again, she pretended a lot more self-confidence and courage than she really felt. "I know we promised no sex."

Brady's midnight-blue eyes narrowed. "That was part of the deal, all right."

"But we had to make it look good," Kelsey persisted as she leapt to her feet once again. Unfortunately, Kelsey thought, it had felt good, too. Much more so than she had expected or ever experienced. But Brady didn't need to know that.

Brady clamped a hand on her shoulder and spun her around to face him. His fingers were as warm and strong as the rest of him, his manner every bit as stubborn and headstrong as hers. "Are we going to have to keep on making it look good?"

Kelsey flushed and stepped back, out of reach. "What do you mean?" she demanded, still able to feel the impression of his touch, even though he was no longer holding on to her.

Brady's eyes narrowed as he reminded her seriously, "Wade McCabe said if our marriage is nothing but a ruse to get his money—which, by the way, we've already taken—then he's going to take the ranch from us."

"I remember," Kelsey said irritably.

"So how are we going to get around that?" Brady adapted a no-nonsense stance, legs braced apart, arms folded in front of him, that would have been very intimidating had Kelsey allowed it.

She didn't. Kelsey ran a hand through her tousled hair, pushing it off her face. "The way I see it, there are all kinds of marriages that are real as can be and yet…well, you know how it is after a while," Kelsey continued as if she knew what she was talking about when she damn well didn't have a clue. "The husband and wife don't seem at all romantic anymore, or even much involved with each other physically, and yet they stay together."

"There's a difference between being together and being happy," Brady pointed out sagely.

"That's true," Kelsey said, "but we could be together and be happy without having sex."

Brady lifted a brow and looked straight into her eyes. "Speak for yourself," he said.

Kelsey stared at him in silence. Brady wasn't sure why he had started this. He just knew someone had to shake up Kelsey's cockeyed view of the world. It looked like it was going to be him. He edged closer. "I don't know any man who is living under the same roof with a woman he lusts after, who is happy when the two of them aren't sleeping together at least every once in a while," Brady continued, and watched the way Kelsey's freckled cheeks turned an even pinker hue.

Kelsey studied him suspiciously as she slightly tilted her pretty head to the side. "Are you saying you lust after me?"

Brady shrugged, seeing no reason to lie about it. Not that he could. Surely, she'd felt his arousal, pressed up against him the way she had been. "After that kiss, I sure do." He hooked his thumbs through the belt loops on either side of his fly and rocked back on his heels. "And now we're going to be living under the same roof."

Kelsey's green eyes shot sparks. "Says who?" she demanded.

"Says me." Brady strode closer. No way was

he going to be her puppet on a string and it was high time she realized that. He lifted a hand and brushed an errant strand of cinnamon-colored hair from her cheek, then cupped her face with his palm. The silky heat of her skin warmed him through and through. "We can't make this look like a real marriage if I'm still sleeping in the stable and you're sleeping in the house."

"Oh. Well." Kelsey jerked in a breath and stepped back, away from him. "You can have one of the other bedrooms, then. There are three to choose from."

Brady knew that would only make things worse. After that kiss, he was going to keep wanting her. And not just as a platonic partner, either. And unless he missed his guess, even if she didn't want to admit it to herself, Kelsey was probably going to keep wanting him, too. "That doesn't solve the problem of lust," he told her frankly, meaning it.

Kelsey knew what he expected here. Like Wade McCabe and everyone else who knew her, Brady expected her to cry uncle, and declare this impetuous marriage of theirs a mistake. Sooner, rather than later. He may have even figured that she would beg Wade McCabe's forgiveness for trying to pull one over on him, and possibly even get it. Well, she wasn't going to do that. People thought she was fickle enough as it was, without adding fuel to the fire. Which left her only one option. Which, under the circumstances, wasn't nearly as untenable an idea as she would have expected it to be.

Kelsey shot Brady a glance, letting him know she was as reckless and impulsive as ever, and proud of it. "Fine then, we'll sleep together once, and then that will be it. At least until we decide it's necessary to do so again. It'll be a good thing," Kelsey continued, picking up steam as she went along. "I'm no good at lying. Everything I feel or think is right on my face, anyway."

Brady rolled his eyes. "No kidding about that," he said dryly.

Kelsey lifted her shoulders in an indifferent shrug and kept her eyes on Brady's. "Now that we're married, everybody is going to be trying to figure out if we've slept together or not, anyway," she told him with as much outrageous brazenness as ever. "So we might as well do it, get it over with, and out of the way, so to speak."

Brady narrowed his eyes at her thoughtfully. To Kelsey's disappointment, he didn't back down one bit, either. "That's a very typically *male* view of things," Brady said, mocking her too-casual tone to a T.

"What?" Kelsey propped her hands on her hips.

The way he was challenging her was making her mad. Worse, it was exciting her, too, in a way unlike anything she'd ever felt before. Stubbornly, she kept her eyes locked with his, even as her heart began to race like a wild thing in her chest. "You don't believe I'm serious?" she asked very softly and coolly.

Brady clamped his lips together. A new, worried light came into his eyes. "I'm not sure what to believe right now," he said seriously, after a moment, suddenly seeming all of his twenty-nine years. "I mean, I know you're a tomboy—"

"Thank you." Kelsey flashed him a tight, mocking smile.

"But this…" Brady continued, clearly at a loss as to what to do next.

Kelsey shot him a sultry smile, already toying with the top button of her shirt. "Don't you want to satisfy your curiosity?" she goaded playfully.

Brady's chest and shoulders suddenly looked hard as rock. "Well, sure…"

Telling herself she didn't need or want to look below his waist, lest she lose her nerve, Kelsey challenged, "Then let's go. Upstairs. Now. You and me."

Brady laughed. Kelsey could see he didn't take her any more seriously than her sisters or the Mc-Cabes. She slowly unbuttoned her shirt and started up the stairs. When she reached the top, she shrugged it off, whirled it lariat-style over her head, and then rocketed it Brady's way.

Brady stared at the shirt fluttering past the stairwell to the floor. The next thing he knew Kelsey had turned the corner into the upstairs hall and a very lacy, surprisingly transparent black bra had followed.

Feeling as if he were in the middle of the wildest, most erotic dream he'd ever had, he moved to pick up the bra. It was still warm from her skin and scented with orange-blossom perfume.

Brady swallowed around the sudden dryness in his throat. Lower still, there was an insistent ache he sure as heck didn't want to be feeling. His fingers closing on the fabric, Brady stared in the direction Kelsey had gone. Damn it all if this new wife of his wasn't serious.

He couldn't believe it.

Not once in the entire time they'd been partners had Kelsey so much as offered him even a handshake. In the space of a few short hours she had proposed marriage, rushed him to city hall, held his hand and kissed him like there was no tomorrow. Now she was taking off her clothes. He swore again as a boot clattered to the first floor. Then another. Then her belt and jeans sailed down from the upstairs hall. A pair of socks followed. Brady swallowed. The only thing she had left was her panties. Before he could even make a move, those followed, too, and they were just as lacy, just as transparent as her bra.

He heard her laughing, then the sound of her footsteps moving toward her bedroom. His lower half surging to life, Brady headed for the stairs.

Kelsey was already beneath the covers in her bedroom. Her cheeks were flushed but there was a telltale devilry in her eyes, and a challenging tilt to her chin. "Are we going to get this over with or not?" she said.

Brady looked at the elegant line of her bare shoulders, and her satiny smooth skin. She had the covers tugged well above her breasts, but what little he could see, coupled with the kiss they had exchanged not too long ago, had him already hard as a rock. "I'm not the kind of guy who plays around," he warned, wanting there to be no mistake about his intentions. "If we do this, if we begin a sexual relationship with each other, there's no going back. I expect exclusive rights to your bedroom and I'll give you the same to mine."

"Fine," Kelsey said as she watched him methodically take off his shirt, boots and jeans. Her pretty green eyes widened as he stripped off his socks and low-slung red briefs, too. "But I reserve the right to say when and where it'll happen."

Brady had no problem with that. Once she was his woman, he figured he could convince her to make love with him anywhere, anytime the need struck. And if not, he thought as a smile curved his mouth, he'd sure have fun trying.

Naked, he climbed beneath the sheets.

To his frustration, although she was naked, too, Kelsey kept her arms on top of the blankets, the covers pressed tightly against her. She had a funny look in her eyes, too. Sort of excited and scared and nervous and yet ridiculously brazen and full of bravado, too. "If I didn't know better," he teased, "I'd think you'd never done this before."

"Ha, ha, very funny." Kelsey gave him a withering look. "Can we just get on with it, please?"

Irritated at the way she kept calling all the shots and ordering him around, Brady frowned. "Sorry for the delay, ma'am." And with that, he lifted the barrier of sheets still between them, shifted over top of her and lowered his head to hers.

The feel of his lips against hers was even more tantalizing and electric than before. Kelsey gasped as Brady's mouth brushed against hers. She quivered all over as he slipped his tongue inside her mouth and rubbed it against hers with lazy, sensual strokes. His hands moved to her breasts, and still kissing her, he shifted his weight, so he was lying beside her, one arm beneath her neck, one leg thrown over hers. When he'd brought her nipples to hot, aching peaks, he let his hand trail lower still, across the flat of her abdomen, and that was when panic, unlike Kelsey had ever felt, set in. Kelsey broke off the kiss and, hands splayed against his chest, pushed him away with all her might. "Stop!" she said. "I can't do this!"

Chapter 3

"What the...?" Brady said, looking every bit as shocked and upset as Kelsey would have expected him to be, given her abrupt change of mind.

"I'm a virgin." Kelsey tugged the covers to her chin and scooted as far away from him as she could without leaving the bed. She hated to disappoint him, but she knew she couldn't go through with it, not feeling the way she did. "I thought I could," she continued, trembling from head to toe. "But I can't. I—" She swallowed hard around the growing ache in her throat. "I'm sorry."

"A virgin," Brady repeated, still looking as

stunned as if she'd hit him over the head with a board.

"Yes." Keeping the sheet wrapped around her like a shield, Kelsey eased from the bed. "So now you know." She took a breath, and kept her eyes from Brady's naked, gloriously sexy body. Doing her best to build on what little dignity she had left, she said, "I trust you won't tell anyone else."

Brady shook his head. "Then what…what was that striptease about?"

"I thought it might be nice to go to bed with you." Kelsey tried her hardest but could not keep her eyes from straying to his long, sturdy limbs and glowing golden skin and the wealth of curly black hair. He was solid muscle from head to toe. And lower still, below his waist… Oh, my. My!

Aware he was still glaring at her, waiting for her to continue, she moved her eyes from his arousal, back to his face. She gulped in great amounts of air. "After all, we're married," she said hastily, wishing he would do something besides lounge there, so expectantly, on her bed. "And it would solve some problems. And…and I've never done it before and all my sisters obviously have, so…"

"So you thought you'd use me to get some experience," Brady said grimly. "And in a roundabout way keep up with all of them." Lips set, he bounded from her bed and snatched up his jeans.

Not about to let him make her into some villainess, when all she had done was make a simple error in judgment, Kelsey stomped closer and shot right back, "Listen, cowboy, it's not like you weren't using me, too. To…to…"

"Experience some pleasure?" Brady filled in the blanks.

"Right." Kelsey tore her eyes from his rigid lower half.

"Only we didn't get anywhere near that, Kelse." Brady stomped closer yet, his strong, tall body exuding so much heat he could practically have started a prairie fire all on his own. "All we did was frustrate ourselves."

Like she didn't know that? She was still tingling all over, still wanting something indescribable, still scared. But she would be damned if she would show Brady Anderson, her new husband, any of that, especially when he was being so sanctimonious. So Kelsey merely went over to her vanity and sat down on the bench. Aware he was watching her every move even as he tugged on his jeans, she crossed her legs at the knee beneath the toga-wrapped sheet, and offered him a sassy smile, pretending an ease she couldn't begin to feel. "Better luck next time?"

"There's not going to be a next time," Brady vowed, grabbing his shirt.

Panic filled Kelsey's soul. She'd gotten used to having Brady around. "What do you mean?" Despite what had just happened between them, she still wanted him in her life.

But, oblivious to her feelings on the matter, Brady jerked on his boots, one after another. "I mean I don't enjoy being played for a fool," he stormed.

"I didn't do that!"

Finished, Brady stood and advanced on her so deliberately and methodically he took her breath away. He didn't stop until he towered over her. "Then what do you call it?" he asked very softly, looking down at her.

Kelsey swallowed but didn't back down. "A mistake."

His lips compressed thinly. "I agree with you there."

Remorse filled her, followed quickly by the need to behave responsibly and make amends. "Brady…"

He put up both hands before she could touch him. "Just don't, Kelse. Just don't."

Without another word, Brady stormed from the room. Kelsey had just started to run after him when the phone rang. Frowning, she went to get it. Rafe Marshall was on the other end of the line. An old school chum of Kelsey's, and former boyfriend, he was now principal at the elementary school and father of eight-year-old twins. "I really need to talk to you," he said. "I've got a big favor to ask. Do you think you could come over to the school and meet me?"

"Now?" She couldn't imagine what Rafe would need to see her about.

"Well, yes," Rafe said, "if it's convenient."

Why not? Kelsey thought, her curiosity piqued. All she was going to do here was sit around and feel bad about what had *not* happened with Brady. "Be right there," Kelsey said.

She went to her closet, put on a fresh set of clothes, retrieved her boots from the bottom of the stairs and headed out the door. She saw Brady come out of the barn just as she was climbing into her pickup truck. Ignoring the way he was looking at her—as if he'd had second thoughts and wanted to talk to her after all—she gunned the truck and sped off.

Rafe was waiting for her when she entered the empty halls. He led her into his office and gestured for her to have a seat. "Shouldn't you be home having dinner with your twins?" Kelsey asked. Since his wife had died a couple of years ago, Rafe had tried to give his kids as much stability as possible. Most nights that meant he was with his kids.

"My mom is visiting and with them. I told her I'd be late." Rafe sank down behind his desk. He was a handsome man, given to wearing his shirts and ties in the exact same color, but the stress of the past few years had left him with wings of gray just above his ears, and at his temples, and a hint of sadness around his eyes. Lately, Kelsey had noted happily, that sadness had been disappearing, bit by bit.

"Kelse, I need your help." As usual, Rafe got straight to the point. "You know Patricia Weatherby?"

Kelsey nodded. "She works at the chamber of commerce, has a little five-year-old girl named Molly." As she recalled, they had stopped in Laramie en route to California when Molly had to have an appendectomy, and liked the town and the people so much they decided to settle here permanently.

"Right. Well—" Rafe paused and drew a deep breath, as if already working up his nerve "—I want to ask her out."

Kelsey shrugged, not sure where she fit into all this. It wasn't as if Rafe needed her permission. The two of them had been over for a long time. "So what's stopping you?" she asked.

"I'm afraid I'll mess it up." Rafe frowned, worry darkening his eyes. "I haven't had a date since I got married and that was years and years ago. I'm afraid if I go out with her, without a little practice, I'll mess it up and blow my chances with Patricia permanently."

Rafe could be a little physically clumsy at times, but Kelsey didn't hold that against him and she couldn't see a nice woman like Patricia Weatherby doing so, either. "You're being a little hard on yourself, aren't you?"

He didn't think so. He picked up a pencil and turned it end over end. "Do you know how many other guys have asked her out since she settled here? Fifteen. No one's made it past a first date. She won't go out with them after that—she says she'd like to be friends, but beyond that, she can tell it's not going to work out. She's real nice about it, from what I've heard, but she's firm. Once she has decided you're not the one for her, you're not the one."

Ouch, Kelsey thought, taking off her cowgirl hat and laying it in her lap.

"And since you sort of operate the same way… Well," Rafe amended quickly when he saw he had offended her. He leaned forward urgently. "You know what I mean. You've dated a lot of guys, Kelsey, and turned 'em all down eventually, usually after just a date or two or three yourself, so…I figured maybe you could clue me in as to what it is exactly that turns women like you and Patricia off to men in the first place. Then I would know what not to do and I could just not do it."

Kelsey could see he was dead serious. "Well, it really isn't any one specific thing, Rafe," she said, being careful not to hurt his feelings, even though she did think he was worrying about this unnecessarily. Still, she figured it wouldn't hurt to help him build up his self-confidence. She sat back in her chair and fingered the brim of her hat. "A lot of things turn a woman off to a guy."

"Such as…?" Rafe pressed.

Kelsey shrugged and did her best to explain. "Sometimes it's a chemistry thing. I get that kiss at the front door at the end of the night, and I know… we haven't got a shot." Unlike with Brady. When he had kissed her, she had known they not only had a shot…that it was damned likely they'd end up together at some point, for at least a certain length of time.

"But it's not always as simple as a lack of chemistry," Rafe said.

"No." With effort, Kelsey forced her mind away from Brady and his kiss, and their near tumble, and back to the conversation at hand. "Sometimes it's the way a guy forgets to open a door for me," she said.

Rafe looked stunned. "*You* want guys to open a door for you?"

"Well, not always. Sometimes. Why?" Kelsey found herself getting defensive. "You got a problem with that?"

"No. I'm just surprised. That's all." Rafe paused. "What else?"

"Well, honestly, Rafe, I don't know." As restless as could be, Kelsey shot out of her chair and paced his office, slapping the brim of her hat against her thigh as she moved. "I haven't even had a date in a while, not since the guys in town stopped asking me out."

"Well, yeah—" Rafe was quick to jump to the other men's defense "—none of them thought they had a chance." He stopped and made a face when he saw he had offended her again. "Sorry. Listen, would you do me a favor? Would you have a secret date with me?"

Kelsey sighed and sat down in her chair again. "Why does it have to be secret?"

"Because I don't want Patricia to think I'm interested in any woman but her when I do ask her out. Besides, what I want you to do is sort of give me a dating lesson. Let's just go somewhere where nobody knows us, and we'll pretend we're on a date, and I'll do all the things I intend to do for Patricia, you know, like holding the door and having dinner table conversation and maybe even asking her to dance if you think that's a good thing. You can critique me. And that'll give me a chance to get all my ducks in a row and build up my confidence before I actually do ask her out. I really, really don't want to blow this, Kelsey. I think Patricia's the woman for me, and I haven't felt that way about a woman since my wife died."

Rafe seemed so sure about what he wanted. Kelsey could only admire him for that. Besides, she figured she owed him. He had steered a lot of kids who wanted riding lessons her way. "I would be happy to help you with that, Rafe," she said.

"How about tomorrow night then?" Rafe asked.

Kelsey hesitated. "Tomorrow's pretty busy. Brady and I are going on a buying trip and I'm not sure how long it will take, or when we'll be back, but Wednesday evening is definitely free."

"Wednesday evening is good for me, too." Rafe smiled. "Meet me at the Gilded Lily, around seven."

Kelsey frowned at the mention of the restaurant he had selected. "There are a couple of waiters over there who are known to be a little snooty, Rafe." In Kelsey's opinion, it was not the place to be if you were as nervous as Rafe was likely to be on his first date with Patricia Weatherby.

"It's also the only true five-star restaurant in

the area and I want to impress Patricia and show her a really memorable time."

Kelsey could see he had his mind made up. Far be it for her to try to change it. "All right, then. The Gilded Lily it is. Oh, and Rafe?" Kelsey paused as she headed out the door. "I probably should mention one more thing. As of this afternoon—I'm married. So your idea about keeping this little dating lesson of ours a secret? It's a good one."

"Where have you been?" Brady demanded the moment Kelsey sauntered in the front door. He was dressed in his usual dusty brown cowboy boots and jeans, but he had changed into a clean blue denim work shirt that brought out the blue of his eyes. Trying not to think what it might be like to go on a date with Brady, Kelsey walked right past him, into the kitchen.

Even though she knew she owed him an apology, she didn't want to think or talk about what had happened between them earlier. She still felt pretty embarrassed at the way she had lured him into her bed and then chickened out at the very last minute, before anything really momentous could happen. But she figured he did not need to know that.

"And hello to you, too, husband dear." Adopting her most carefree air, Kelsey put the bag containing a take-out beef barbecue dinner down on the table. "I hope you're hungry. I bought this especially for you."

His scowl faded as the aroma of tender, mesquite-flavored beef and spicy barbecue sauce filled the air. "If you'd have asked me, I'd have gone with you."

Kelsey brought out containers of vinegar-based slaw, potato salad and beans, and snapped the lids off those, too. She held his gaze for a moment, before she went to get the plates and silverware. "I thought we both needed some cooling-off time."

"You can say that again." Brady brought two cold drinks and a stack of paper napkins to the table and held out a chair for her before he sat himself. As casually as if they ate dinner as a couple every day. If she didn't know better, she'd think he'd been talking to Rafe about the things she really wanted from a man. One thing was for sure. Brady'd never held a door or chair for her before, not even when they got married this afternoon. In fact, he'd gone out of his way to steer physically clear of her.

Kelsey waited until they had both filled their plates with a generous amount of food, then said, "Listen. About what happened earlier, I'm sorry."

Brady sighed in a way that let her know he had

as many regrets as she did. He reached across the table and took both her hands in his. "I'm sorry, too." He looked at her deliberately. "I scared you and I sure didn't mean to do that. If you'd just told me you were a beginner..." His voice trailed off.

Despite her desire to remain in peace-making mode, Kelsey couldn't help the rise of temper insider her belly. He made her sound so inept. She tugged her hands out of his. "A beginner?"

"A beginner in bed," Brady corrected himself hastily. "Okay?"

Kelsey frowned. She hated the fact he looked so at ease when she was still tied up in knots. "Well, if I am, it's not for lack of trying this afternoon."

"If I had known how inexperienced you were," Brady huffed in an irritated tone of voice Kelsey was beginning to know all too well, "I would have said no."

Kelsey rolled her eyes. "Exactly why I didn't tell you," Kelsey sassed right back, determined not to let him get the better of her in this or any other way.

"But had I agreed," Brady added as if she hadn't spoken, continuing to look at her in a very sexy, very determined way, "I would have indoctrinated you slowly. I wouldn't have rushed you into it. I would have—"

"Seduced me?" Kelsey guessed hopefully as the two of them began to eat.

"Yes." Brady nodded.

Abruptly, Kelsey's mind was filled with images of the two of them in bed. All night. "Well, we could still do that," Kelsey murmured offhandedly, her curiosity mounting as her innate recklessness took over once again and pushed her to explore this life to its limits. What would it have been like, she wondered, if she hadn't panicked, but instead had regained her courage and let Brady's hand move lower, more intimately still? Would he have made love to her, the way he had wanted to make love to her? Would they still be in her bed now? Despite her fear, she tingled just thinking about the possibility of losing her virginity with Brady. Here. Now. Tonight. After all, he was her husband....

Brady, who was still watching her intently, guessed at the nature of her thoughts and made a rude, guffawing sound in the back of his throat. "Oh, no, Kelse. Not on your life are we trying that again."

Kelsey's brows knitted together in consternation. The disaster this afternoon aside, she had never been one to give up on anything she really wanted, and neither, she sensed, had Brady.

"Why not?" she asked. Wasn't that what you

were supposed to do when you fell off a horse, so to speak? Get back on?

Brady took a thirsty gulp of his drink and forked up some tender beef. "Because I am not all that fond of sexual torture and cold showers, that's why not."

Kelsey watched him chow down for several long seconds. "That's what it felt like to you?" she asked after a moment. "Torture?"

Brady rolled his eyes and gave her an annoyed look. "Honey, hours later, I'm still hard. And I figure I'm going to be that way for a while."

Kelsey was glad the tabletop obstructed her view of his lap. Otherwise, she might have been tempted to look to see if that was, quite literally, true. One thing was certain—this discussion they were having looked like it was making him as physically uncomfortable as it was making her. She paused and wet her lips, then asked curiously, "Is that natural, for you to still be…?"

Brady silenced her with a hand to her lips. "Please," he groaned out loud, as if he were in pain. "No more questions. And no more talk of us going to bed together because it is just not going to happen," he said firmly.

Now that Kelsey was getting her nerve back, she was beginning to get excited all over again. She hated being excited about something with no opportunity for follow-through. And her feminine instinct told her that if the time and place were right, Brady could show her a very good time. She thrust her lower lip at him contentiously. "I think you're being unfair." Maybe this could work out after all. Given a little time and a lot more tutoring and patience on his part. "Couldn't we just, um, experiment a little, see where things lead?"

Brady sighed and looked as if he were praying for patience. "Didn't anyone ever tell you not to play with fire, Kelse? You might get burned."

That was just it, Kelsey thought, she wanted to get burned—by Brady. Before either of them could say anything further, there was a knock at the front door. "I'll get it." Looking relieved at the interruption, Brady bolted from the room.

Her mood glum, Kelsey stayed where she was. Seconds later, Kelsey heard the front door open. Then voices—both male and female. Too soon, Brady was back in the kitchen, Kelsey's sister Dani and her husband, Beau, with him.

"Can you believe it?" the six months pregnant Dani was saying, as she set down a small wedding cake from Isabelle Buchanon's bakery. "Tonight of all nights, our plumbing goes out. Sorry, Kelse. Beau and I are just going to have to sleep here at the ranch with you and Brady tonight. I hope you don't mind."

How naive did people think she and Brady were? Kelsey wondered. Even a five-year-old could have seen through a ploy like this. "Would it matter if I did mind?" Kelsey asked Dani facetiously.

"I know you've had a busy day, although I was surprised to see that you and Brady didn't exactly spend it all together. I saw you getting out of your truck over at the school earlier this evening. You were alone." Dani spoke as if that were a grave indictment of the marriage already.

"I'm not alone now," Kelsey said, refusing to explain what she had been doing at the school. "And if you want to know the truth, you and Beau are interrupting our first night as man and wife."

"Well, you could always put it off then until you are alone," Dani said blithely, as if that were the best idea in the whole wide world. "Just sleep in separate bedrooms tonight," she advised with a smile. "Brady at one end of the hall. You at the other. Beau and me in my old room, in between. Perfect."

Kelsey looked at Beau, Dani's husband. He was never this quiet, except when it came to family conflicts. Then, he tended to step back and let the sisters work out their problems largely unassisted. "How did you get dragged into this?" Kelsey asked Beau.

Beau flashed her his movie-star grin. "I know when Lockhart fireworks are coming up. Figured I'd be here to keep the peace. Besides, we can't sleep at our house tonight, remember? Anyway—" Beau shot a look at both Kelsey and Brady, as if trying to decide for himself if this marriage was a hoax or not "—I hope the two of us aren't imposing too much."

Kelsey could see that was true. Beau, who'd only been a member of the family a short time, was willing to give both Kelsey and Brady the benefit of the doubt, as well as a chance to make things work. Her usually a-lot-more-understanding older sister harbored no such generosity.

Kelsey gritted her teeth and hung on to her temper with effort. "It really isn't necessary to chaperone us, you know," she said evenly after a moment. She stood and fit her hand into Brady's much larger one, loving the way his callused fingers immediately closed around hers. "I'm perfectly safe here at the ranch with Brady," Kelsey continued, without an ounce of her usual recklessness. "He's a good guy."

"I don't doubt that at all," Beau said firmly, giving Brady a man-to-man glance that seemed to speak volumes.

"He's not going to do anything to hurt me," Kelsey added firmly.

"I'm quite aware of that," Dani countered, catching the brunt of Kelsey's withering glare. "It's your own impulsiveness that is the problem."

Kelsey frowned, her urge to throw a full-fledged temper tantrum growing. "What's that supposed to mean?" she demanded icily.

Dani sighed and put a gentle hand on Kelsey's shoulder. "Honey, I know how competitive you are, but this is not the way to go about catching up with the rest of us."

"Don't even start." Kelsey pushed her sister away. "What do you know." She shook her head at the half-finished meal on the table. "I've lost my appetite." She stormed away from the table, pausing only long enough to look at Dani. "You know where the sheets are." As far as Kelsey was concerned, her uninvited chaperones could make up their own bed. "Meanwhile," she continued stormily, ignoring the thick silence that had fallen over the room, "I'm going on to bed. And Brady—" Kelsey looked at him long and hard, letting him know this was one loyalty test she expected him to pass with flying colors "—I expect you to join me."

Chapter 4

"Well, isn't this cozy," Brady said, joining Kelsey in the master bedroom a few minutes later, shaving kit in hand.

Trying not to feel self-conscious in the ribbed knit undershirt and loose-fitting men's pajama pants she typically wore to bed, Kelsey went into the adjoining bathroom and plucked her toothbrush out of the holder. "Don't look at me like it's all my fault," she warned as she squeezed toothpaste onto the brush.

Brady tossed his shaving kit onto the counter next to her orange-blossom shampoo. "Isn't it?" Arms folded in front of him, Brady lounged in the doorway and watched her brush, rinse and spit. His lips set, he unzipped his bag and pulled out his own toothbrush and paste. "You could have done what your sister so clearly wanted you to do and offered to put off our *wedding night* until we were alone."

"Which is going to be never, in case you haven't figured that out," Kelsey whispered back, pausing to blot her mouth with a towel. Unable to get by him, because his tall frame was blocking the only exit out of the small bath, she bided her time impatiently as Brady brushed his teeth.

Able to see he still didn't understand what was really going on here, Kelsey continued to whisper, "Ten to one, Meg and Luke, and Jenna and Jake, would be here, too, if they didn't have kids at home. But they do. So obviously Dani and Beau have been elected—"

"—or volunteered," Brady interrupted, following his tooth-brushing with a swish of mouthwash.

"—to play chaperone for me and you," Kelsey finished haughtily.

Brady straightened and gave her a look. "Maybe it's not such a bad idea, given what they think is the reason you married me today." He led the way back into the bedroom.

Kelsey stormed after him. "I am not competing with them!"

He turned to face her and continued unbutton-ing his shirt. "Not even a tiny little bit?" he de-manded, towering over her.

"Well, okay." Reminded of what had happened, or nearly happened between them that afternoon, Kelsey backed up a step. She swallowed hard around the sudden parched feeling in her throat and forced herself to look up at him as if being here with him like this did not bother her in the least. "I wouldn't mind it if I had already found the love of my life, but I haven't so…" She let the thought go unfinished. Then, deciding she was much too close to him, she went around to her side of the bed and climbed in.

Looking unhappier than ever, Brady stripped off his shirt, boots and jeans, and climbed in be-side her. "So you 'made do' with me," he theo-rized grimly.

Unwilling to lie down just yet, now that they were actually in bed together again, Kelsey propped herself against the headboard. She pulled the sheet up to her chest and held it against her breasts. "That isn't it and you know it."

Brady gave her a hard look that challenged her veracity as he settled back against the headboard, too.

"We're partners," Kelsey continued stubbornly.

Brady tugged the covers no higher than his

waist. "And man and wife," he muttered in a low, disgruntled tone that carried no further than their bed, "who—thanks to your impulsiveness—are now sharing a bed for the night."

"What choice did we have?" Kelsey railed right back at him in the same highly irascible manner. "If I'd not slept in the same room and the same bed with you tonight," she shot back quietly, "then Dani and Beau might have told Wade McCabe there was nothing to worry about after all. Wade would have concluded that this wasn't a real marriage, and there goes the deed to the ranch." Still holding on to the covers, she clamped her arms in front of her and stared straight ahead. "I am not giving up this ranch."

"Well, there we agree, anyway," Brady said, abruptly lying down and stretching out beside her.

Was it her imagination, Kelsey wondered, or was this bedroom of hers getting smaller and more intimate by the minute? Beside her, Brady shifted around and sighed loudly. Kelsey rolled her eyes and refused to look at him. "Now what's wrong?" she whispered stonily.

Brady shifted again. His shoulders were so broad, they took up his half of the bed, and his legs were so long, his feet were hanging off the end of the mattress. He grimaced and continued to try to get comfortable. "This bed is awfully small."

Kelsey shifted a little farther away from him, so they would no longer be touching, and nearly fell off the edge of the bed. He was making this harder than it had to be, she thought, glaring at him. "It's a double." It should sleep two.

"Which would be fine for me alone," Brady conceded, sighing and staring at the ceiling again, "but with you in here…it's going to be awfully darn hard to sleep here without touching each other."

"So what if we do touch each other?" Kelsey challenged. "Nothing's going to happen we don't want to happen. Unless—" Kelsey paused, grinning, as the next idea—and it was a brilliant one—hit.

As the silence strung out between them, Brady rolled toward her. "What?" Brady demanded suspiciously, searching her face.

Kelsey shifted onto her side to face him. She snapped her fingers and flashed him a mischievous grin. "Never fear, cowboy. I know how to get rid of Beau and Dani faster than you can say 'We're outta here!'"

Brady did not like that look in Kelsey's vibrant green eyes. That look always guaranteed trouble. "What are you up to now?" he demanded.

Kelsey raised her knees beneath the covers,

braced her arms on either side of her, and began to rock back and forth suggestively. "Let's see how loud we can get this bed to squeak."

Brady swore, rolled and grabbed her shoulders, hard enough to temporarily stop her. "Are you out of your mind?" he said, ignoring the tantalizing warmth of her skin beneath his fingertips.

"No." The flush in Kelsey's cheeks increased and the soft edges of her lips curled up merrily. "Actually, if you want to know the truth—" she paused and waggled her eyebrows at him teasingly "—when it comes to bright ideas, I'm 'in the zone' today."

Brady ignored the clear definition of her breasts beneath the clinging blue cotton undershirt. Kelsey might not realize how sexy she looked, dressed for bed, but he did, and it was driving him crazy. The last thing he needed was her emulating the sounds of the two of them making love. "That is definitely a matter of opinion," he said, pushing away images of their erotically entwined bodies.

Kelsey scowled at him. As the seconds drew out, her lips formed a delicious pout. "It makes perfect sense," she countered in that soft, determined tone he knew so well. "And if you would just stop and think a minute, Brady, you would know that."

Deciding holding her that way was courting danger, Brady let her go and shifted away from her.

Kelsey sighed and elaborated in a low, exasperated voice. "Dani and Beau are here to prevent us from making love, if we haven't already done so."

"So?" Brady said.

"So—" Kelsey frowned at him impatiently, looking as if she were irked that she was still having to explain her thinking to him. "The two of them would be here with us until their baby was born if they thought they could prevent our consummating our marriage with their mere presence."

Given the possessive, protective way he was beginning to feel about Kelsey, maybe that wasn't such a bad idea, Brady thought.

"I love my sister and her new husband," Kelsey continued to explain resolutely, looking Brady square in the eye, "but I don't want them in residence with me for the next three months."

Put that way, neither did Brady. Although, up until this afternoon, he and Kelsey had been only business partners, he had come to relish his time alone with her.

"Now, on the other hand," Kelsey theorized softly, with a very wicked grin, "if my nosy sister and her husband discover we're already making love, the horse is already out of the barn. There would be nothing they could do to invalidate our marriage, and they'd likely leave. So what we need to do, fast, is make it sound like we're making hot and heavy love in here. So come on," Kelsey whispered, pausing to utter a long, sultry moan that swiftly had Brady groaning softly, too—for a completely different reason. "Help me here," she whispered as she began to rock back and forth.

For a virgin, she was remarkably adept at simulating the sounds of lovemaking. Too adept for Brady's comfort. The hard-on he'd had earlier sprang back to life, with near painful consequences. He knew much more of this and they'd both have reason to regret her impetuousness. She thought she'd been shocked before...

"Cut it out, Kelsey," Brady warned grimly.

"No." Kelsey threw her head back against the pillows, exposing the long slender column of her throat and, beneath the scooped neckline of her undershirt, the tempting uppermost curves of her breast and the jutting imprints of her nipples. Shutting her eyes, she rocked all the harder and moaned again, even louder. Down the hall, he could hear the sounds of Dani and Beau moving around, stepping out into the hall.

Brady knew he had to stop her—now. Before her sister and husband came to investigate, and discovered this for the ruse it all was. Because she wasn't about to *listen* to him, there was only one way to do that.

Brady moved swiftly, so he was on top of her. As abruptly as his weight covered hers, she went still. The sultry moan came to a strangled end as her green eyes opened wide. She looked first startled, then furious as—unable to rock the bed even the slightest, with his weight stopping her—she moaned again, even louder, and whispered feistily, "You're not stopping me."

"The heck I'm not," Brady threatened, and then he quickly shut her up the only way he knew how. He lowered his lips to hers and delivered a traffic-stopping kiss.

She uttered another moan of strangled passion, and then to Brady's dismay, instead of stiffening in shocked resistance—the way he expected her to—or trying to fight him off, she wreathed her arms around his neck, opened her mouth to the plundering pressure of his, and let her body melt against his. He thought kissing her earlier, in this bed, when they'd both been naked and willing as could be, had been arousing. It was nothing compared to the way he felt now. His body ignited. And so did his soul. Despite the reckless way she had behaved all day, baiting him and driving him crazy, he wanted her. Damn, how he wanted her...

Kelsey had known, after the way she had panicked earlier, that Brady expected her to fight him off. Which was, precisely, why she hadn't. She didn't want him thinking he could second-guess her, when the truth was, he just couldn't. And… she had also had all day to think about what she had walked out on when she had cut and run from this bed. Fiery kisses. Heart-stopping passion. Not to mention the possibility of actually climaxing for the first time in her life. It infuriated her to realize she was as old as she was, and still had no earthly idea what all the fuss was about. If all the romantic books and movies, not to mention the glowing happiness of all three of her sisters, were anything to go by, what she had been missing up to now was pretty darn sensational.

But not as sensational as the feeling of Brady's lips, moving over hers, or the intoxicating pressure of his tongue twining with hers. He tasted hot, male and forbidden. He smelled even better—like soap and cologne. His body was warm, strong, solid. And the way he was pressing against her created a delicious, tingling ache.

The fear she'd felt earlier gone, Kelsey gave herself over to the steamy embrace completely. And that was when Brady stopped, lifted his head and swore again.

* * *

"Dammit," Brady whispered, rolling onto his back, his every muscle—and he had a lot of them—tensed and flexed. "I told you we were not going to do this, Kelsey."

Trembling, Kelsey stared at him. "I don't see why not," she told him breathlessly.

"Obviously." Brady shut his eyes and lay his arm across his forehead.

Kelsey rolled onto her side and studied him in the dim bedroom light. Despite the fact it was rather cool in there, a light sheen of sweat had broken out on his body. He was breathing as hard as if he'd just run a six-kilometer race at top speed. "Are you okay?" she asked after a moment. She thought she was all worked up, given the way her body was tingling and aching with frustration, but Brady almost looked as if he were in pain.

Brady swore again, not moving in the slightest. "If I head for the shower, will they be able to hear the water running from down the hall?" he asked.

Kelsey thought a minute. "Yeah."

Brady swore again.

Kelsey brightened. "I could go with you," she offered. "You know, talk and moan a lot. If they thought we were in there together, it wouldn't look so suspicious. In fact, from what I gather, showering together is a pretty newlywed thing to do. So…"

Brady groaned again, even more miserably than before. To Kelsey's consternation, rather than take her up on her rather brilliant suggestion, he reached over and turned off the light. Dropping back onto the pillows, he continued breathing as if he were in dire pain. "Kelsey?"

"Hmm?"

"Stay on your side of the bed," he ordered gruffly. "Be quiet. And go to sleep."

Kelsey had never been one to take orders, but something in Brady's voice told her she had better do what he said. So she turned onto her side, away from him, and tried not to think about what had almost happened, what most certainly would have happened, had she not chickened out earlier that day.

The next thing she knew it was morning, there were sounds of people moving around downstairs, and Brady was nowhere in sight. Trying not to feel disappointed she hadn't gotten to see what it would be like to wake with him sleeping next to her, she got up, pulled on a robe over her pajamas and headed downstairs. To her surprise, Brady was at the stove, cooking breakfast for Beau and Dani as if he owned the place. Which, Kelsey had to admit reluctantly, now that they were married, he sort of did.

"Morning." Brady smiled at her as if absolutely nothing had happened before.

Kelsey resented him for that. She had expected him to act as physically frustrated and out of sorts as she was. But maybe it was better that he didn't, she decided quickly, given the fact they had a very nosy audience who were intently watching everything she and Brady did and said. "Morning." Kelsey nodded at Brady, then at Dani and Beau. Since when had the three of them become such good friends? she wondered suspiciously.

"Pancakes or eggs?" Brady asked.

"Both," Kelsey said, just to be obstinate.

"Coming right up." Brady turned back to the stove.

"Brady was just telling us he thought it would be okay if I did some location shots here for the movie I'm working on," Beau said. "Is it okay with you? The film company would pay you for the use of your cattle and horses and pastures, of course."

"Of course." Kelsey nodded, feeling like a fool because this method of making money to further expand the ranch hadn't occurred to her before.

Dani smiled, looking a lot more at ease with Kelsey's marriage to Brady than she had the night before. To Kelsey's further aggravation, breakfast continued, pleasant as could be, with Brady playing the cheerful host, and Beau and Dani talking up the new film project Beau was working on and the recent movie reviews she had written, plus the book of movie reviews Dani was about to publish, until it was finally time for them to head to their respective offices.

"I imagine our plumbing will be fixed this evening," Beau announced as he exchanged a meaningful glance with Dani. Dani nodded, too, and Beau continued, "So we won't be coming back tonight. You two lovebirds will be on your own."

Thank heavens, Kelsey thought. But for once did not speak her mind.

Dani and Beau left. Kelsey slapped her hands on her hips and turned on Brady. She hated being protected or excluded and it looked like the three of them had just done both. "Just what the heck did you tell them before I woke up?" she said.

Brady looked her right in the eye. "The truth. That I'd cut off my right arm before I'd do anything to hurt you," he said quietly.

The wind went out of Kelsey's sails as quickly as it had come in. "Well, apparently they bought it hook, line and sinker," Kelsey said as she finished her coffee in a single gulp.

"I mean it." Brady took her by the shoulders

and held her in front of him. The truth of what he was saying was in his midnight-blue eyes. "You're not just my partner now, you're my wife, Kelse. We're building something pretty darn important here and I don't want to lose that."

Kelsey swallowed around the sudden lump of emotion in her throat. "I don't, either," Kelsey said cautiously. To her amazement, she felt oddly protective of him, too.

"Good." Brady nodded as if that settled that. To Kelsey's disappointment, he stepped back and returned his attention to the eggs cooking on the stove. "Now that we've got money in the bank, I think it might be a good time for us to go and look at those additional horses and ponies you've been wanting to buy, and put a bid in on some more tack for your riding stables." He filled two plates with eggs and pancakes, and then sat down at the table with her.

Kelsey realized without wanting to that she could quickly get used to taking all her meals with Brady. Maybe even sleeping with him, too. Not that she needed to be thinking about that at all, given the fact he had chosen not to make love to her the previous night, even when she had changed her mind and said it would be okay.

She swallowed around the sudden parched feeling in her throat, and tried to think about business instead of the incredibly wonderful and satisfying way Brady kissed. "We can get a better deal on some used tack if we go to the auction house," she said, as if their business were all she had on her mind.

"Good idea," Brady said as he added butter and syrup to his stack of fluffy golden hotcakes. "I want to cut our expenses as much as possible to make room in the budget for the cowboys I'm intending to hire."

Kelsey noted he needed to shave. She liked the way he looked with a morning beard, sort of dark and dangerous, maybe even a little bit like an outlaw. A very handsome, sexy outlaw. Aware she was letting her thoughts digress again into forbidden territory, Kelsey forced herself to straighten up and get her mind out of the bedroom. It was funny, what a little thing like a marriage license and ceremony could do to a woman—even a formerly nonromantic tomboy like herself. She'd been married to Brady less than a day, and already she could feel herself changing—for the better.

"When will that be?" she asked, aware she wasn't looking forward to a time when she and Brady would no longer inhabit the ranch alone.

"As soon as I can find qualified cowhands and staff up," Brady told her, looking as if he were longing for that day as much as she was dreading it. "I asked them to put up a Help Wanted sign for me at the feed store and also posted a notice with the Cattle Raisers Association. Hopefully, calls about working for me won't be long in coming."

Chapter 5

Brady finished the dishes and threw some corn in his pickup and drove out to feed the twenty head of Black Angus cattle he already had while Kelsey showered and got ready to go. When she came downstairs, he was still out on the ranch somewhere. But there was an older man she had never seen before walking around their front yard. He was standing next to a late-model luxury sedan. He had on an elegant suit that was very much at odds with his craggy, rough-hewn appearance. Frowning, Kelsey went out to see who he was and what he wanted. As she got closer, he swept off his dove-gray cowboy hat, revealing a full head of silver hair that was badly in need of a trim.

"Can I help you?"

He nodded at her politely and put his hat back on his head, before striding toward her authoritatively. His dark eyes zeroed in on hers. "I'm looking for Brady Anderson or Kelsey Lockhart," he said in a raspy voice.

"I'm Kelsey." Kelsey held out her hand—it was immediately swallowed up in his much larger, very callused palm. "What can I do for you?" she continued, noting the expensive gold rings he had on each hand. The diamond, onyx and ruby stones looked to be genuine and expensive. Not the kind of thing an ordinary cowpoke or someone from Laramie, Texas, would wear. The same went for his shiny alligator boots.

"My name is Hargett," he said.

"Pleased to meet you," Kelsey said. Was it her imagination or was their unexpected caller giving her a particularly close—almost suspicious— scrutiny, too?

Before Kelsey could ask Hargett anything more, Brady roared back into the yard. He jumped out of his truck and strode toward them. It was clear by the extremely irked look on Brady's handsome face that he knew who Hargett was even if she didn't. "What are you doing here?" Brady demanded, ignoring Kelsey and going straight for Hargett.

"Nothing yet," Kelsey said, not sure why Brady was being so rude to this man.

Ignoring her, Brady looked at Hargett. "We had a deal," he stated tightly, abruptly looking like he wanted to punch someone or something. "You weren't to come near me."

Hargett shrugged, not the least bit apologetic. "Time's up," he said.

Brady clenched his jaw and, still glaring at Hargett resentfully, pushed the words through his teeth, "Not for two more weeks it's not."

Brady wheeled around abruptly. Putting his hands on her shoulders, he propelled her toward the ranch house. "Kelsey, wait inside."

Kelsey's jaw dropped open at the unprecedented autocratic timbre of Brady's tone. She dug in her heels obstinately and refused to comply with his rude order. She glared at Brady. If there was something going on here, she wanted to know what it was. "You don't tell me what to do!" she spouted off.

Brady was not in the least amused by her rebellious attitude, but Hargett chuckled. "I like a gal with spunk," he said.

Brady shot Hargett a lethal look before turning back to Kelsey. "In this case," he countered firmly, "I am telling you what to do." When she still refused to budge, Brady took Kelsey by the arm and led her to the porch steps, well out of earshot of Hargett, who was still sending them both interested looks. "This doesn't concern you."

Kelsey arched a warning brow of her own. "Need I remind you that we are partners and as such everything you do on this ranch concerns me?"

"This doesn't." Brady enunciated each syllable in a way that had Kelsey's own temper flaring sky-high. "Now, go inside and wait for me there." He waited, expecting her to do his bidding. Kelsey still didn't budge. "Fine," Brady said, swearing beneath his breath. "Hargett and I will just leave and have our conversation elsewhere."

Exasperated by Brady's unexpected secretive-ness, Kelsey blew out a gusty breath. "You don't have to do that. I'll go inside," she grumbled ill-temperedly, figuring at least she could spy on them and gather what information she could that way.

"Thank you," Brady said, clearly hanging on to his patience by a thread.

Kelsey rolled her eyes and stomped off. She didn't know what was going on, but she did not like the way Brady was behaving. He was going to pay for this.

* * *

Brady waited until Kelsey was safely in the ranch house before he walked back to Hargett. Then, moving so they were on the other side of the pickup truck and facing away from the windows, Brady stated roughly, with what precious little patience he had left, "You shouldn't have come here."

Hargett shook his head at Brady sadly. "That sweet little wife of yours doesn't know anything about the deal you made with me, does she?"

"No." Brady tensed as he thought about what would happen if he couldn't follow through on his half of the bargain he had made. "And I don't want her to know, either." Brady paused, wondering how best to protect Kelsey from the choices he had made in his desperate attempt to change his life for the better. Now that he thought about it, he should have realized Hargett would show up here as soon as he learned about the marriage. But he hadn't thought about it, because he hadn't really wanted to face the fact that this day of reckoning was coming, and soon, whether he liked it or not. Brady blew out a short, restless breath. "How did you know we were married, anyway?" Brady searched Hargett's face.

Hargett took a cigar out of his pocket and lit the end of it. "My people do a search of the state records every day." He paused to draw on the end of it, then put the lighter away. "Your name came up on a marriage license yesterday. When they brought it to my attention, I figured I had better check it out."

Brady sighed and rubbed the tense muscles in the back of his neck. "Yeah, well, I wish you hadn't." He shot a look at the window, and saw Kelsey standing there in plain view. Brady's frown deepened as he realized his wife was taking in everything she could about his little set-to with Hargett. "Now she's going to be full of questions," Brady complained.

Hargett took another long drag on his cigar. "Perhaps rightly so, if she's your wife."

Brady fell silent. He refused to feel guilty about keeping his past from Kelsey. What was important was not the life he had been born into or the man he had been, but the man he was now.

"She has a right to know about your past, Brady," Hargett insisted.

"I'll tell her when the time is right," Brady retorted stubbornly, "and not before."

Hargett studied Brady, as always seeing far more about what Brady was thinking and feeling than Brady wanted. "In two weeks—" he began.

"I'll have met my conditions for my freedom," Brady interrupted.

"If not, you know you're going to have to come back to work for me," Hargett said sternly. Still puffing away on his cigar, he inclined his head toward the ranch house. "A deal is a deal whether you are married to that pretty gal or not."

Brady waited until Hargett had left before he headed for the ranch house. He walked in to find Kelsey sitting in a chair, her arms behind her, a bandanna drawn like a gag across her mouth. He raced to her side and tugged it off. "What happened?" he demanded worriedly.

Lazily, Kelsey brought her hands—which were not tied after all—around to her lap. "Oh, I can talk now?" she queried innocently.

Too late, Brady wished his "gag order" had stayed in effect.

He rubbed at the back of his neck again. "I'm sorry I had to order you inside like that," he said.

"Are you?" Kelsey repeated in the same mocking tone.

"I didn't want you talking to him," Brady continued, doing his best to appease her while at the same time telling her as little as possible.

"That was apparent." Kelsey studied him. Slowly she rose from her chair to square off with him, a little less hot-temperedly. "Who is Mr. Hargett, anyway?"

Good question. And one I am not about to answer all the way. At least not right before I get my permanent release from his service worked out with him, Brady thought. "I used to work for him," he said finally, telling her as much as he could, without abruptly ruining the rapport he and Kelsey had built up over the five months they had known each other and the four months they had been partners.

"As a cowhand?" Kelsey asked pointedly, still scrutinizing his face.

Brady shrugged, uncomfortable with lying to Kelsey or anyone else even a little bit, but not willing to divulge the complete truth to her or anyone else, either. The life he'd had in the past was over. He didn't live that way anymore. Unfortunately, his past wouldn't remain in the shadows if he started talking about it to anyone who was curious. "More of a jack-of-all-trades," he allowed eventually, telling her only what he was comfortable with.

"And you quit," Kelsey guessed.

"Yes."

Kelsey's brows knit together, her expression perplexed. "Why?"

Brady sighed, wishing like heck this new wife of his was not so persistent. "Because I didn't like what I was doing for him," Brady explained.

"Why not?"

"Because I wasn't suited for what he wanted me to do." Brady tried but could not quite keep the exasperation from his low voice.

"Then why did he show up here today?" Kelsey continued, moving even closer to Brady. She didn't stop until they were toe-to-toe. "Does he want you to work for him again?"

"Yes," Brady said firmly, as he drank in the clean and sexy orange-blossom smell of her hair and skin, "but I'm not going to do that."

The soft edges of Kelsey's lips turned up in a slight smile. "So why couldn't I hear you tell him that?" she asked casually.

It was all Brady could do not to roll his eyes and/or beg for mercy. "Because Hargett and I don't get along all that well. He's a pretty blunt-spoken man and there's never any telling what he's going to say. I didn't want you to be witness to any unpleasantness."

Kelsey thought about that for a minute. "And that's all it was."

"Yes." He had been protecting his wife from Hargett's pushiness, plain and simple. She hadn't been in any physical danger. But she could easily have had her heart broken—had Hargett had more of a chance to disillusion her by telling her everything Brady had not.

Brady had known he was going to have to tell her all he'd done and why, for a while now. But he had wanted to wait until his past debts were cleared and they had money in the bank. That would not happen for another two weeks.

"So I wasn't in danger," Kelsey said.

Brady frowned. It was time this conversation took another tack. "Only from me," he teased her lightly, "if you don't stop talking."

Kelsey rolled her eyes. "You are one of the most difficult men I have ever met."

Doing what he had wanted to do from the first moment he had laid eyes on her that morning, Brady wrapped his arms around her. "The same goes for you in the female category."

Kelsey narrowed her eyes at him as she splayed her hands across his chest. She tilted her head up, to better search his face. "I know you're not telling me everything," she insisted worriedly.

Brady could feel her body melting against him, even while her will remained as feisty and difficult as ever. He grinned as he realized he wanted her to surrender to him heart and soul. Pushing her hair back away from her face, he brushed his thumb across her lips and told her softly, "A little mystery is good for every marriage, haven't you heard?"

"Brady—"

He kissed her deliberately, rubbing his lips across hers, then with growing intensity, until nothing was held in check. He had counted on her mouth to be soft and sweet. He hadn't expected her to rise up on tiptoe, thread her hands through his hair, press her slender body against his and kiss him back passionately, wildly, wantonly. He could feel the surrender of her body in the trembling of her knees, and the way her soft, delicate hands caressed his shoulders with slow, seductive strokes. And yet there remained an innocence to her as she met him boldly, kiss for kiss. He wished he could take her upstairs and make up for the calamity that had happened the day before, when she had lured him there unexpectedly. But he knew he couldn't do that.

Reluctantly, Brady drew back. There would be time for more kisses. Maybe even time for wooing her and making her his woman, as well as his wife. But it wouldn't be this morning. Not when they still had so much work to be done, a ranch to outfit, and only two weeks to finish making this ranch the roaring success he knew it could be. He let his arms fall to his sides and stepped back. Ignoring the faint but unmistakable look of disappointment on Kelsey's face, he tugged the brim of his hat low across his brow, so it shadowed his eyes from her searching gaze, and said, "We better go if we're going to look at those horses and ponies today."

Fortunately for both of them, the schedule of appointments they had made for that morning kept them plenty busy. There was no more time for kisses. Only serious looking and hard bargaining. "No way are we paying that price for those horses," Brady said, when they finally found what they wanted, midafternoon. He stepped forward to negotiate with the owner, a crafty man who reminded him very much of his former "boss."

"They're worth every penny," the rancher said.

"Individually," Brady concurred, before Kelsey could give in and just agree to pay the owner the inflated price he wanted. "Since we're taking them all off your hands at once, saving you all that time, effort and feed, we should get a better deal."

The rancher shrugged indifferently. "The price stands."

Beside him, Kelsey tensed. Brady remained unconcerned. He knew a bluff when he saw one. "Then we go to the next ranch on the list," Brady said, taking Kelsey's arm.

"Okay, okay, wait," the rancher said before they could depart. "I'll lower the price by five percent."

"Twenty," Brady insisted.

"Ten," the rancher countered, frowning.

"Twelve and we'll call it a deal," Brady said.

The rancher sighed. "Done." He shook hands with Brady, then Kelsey. They talked about the transfer of the horses, which would be done in forty-eight hours, and completed the bill of sale. In silence, they walked back to Brady's pickup truck to go to the auction house and look at the used saddles and bridles that had come in from a ranch west of there.

"I could have handled the negotiations on my own, you know," Kelsey said as soon as Brady turned back onto the highway.

Brady knew Kelsey was irritated with him, and for good reason from her perspective. She was an equal partner, and hence should have had fifty percent of the say in what was going on. Knowing by the look on her face, however, that she was going to cost them money they didn't have to spend if he let her in on the bargaining, he had cut her out of the negotiations. Brady was sorry he had hurt her feelings. He wasn't sorry for the business stance he had taken. "You were ready to just give him the money he wanted, and I knew he'd take less," Brady said.

Kelsey scowled. "But if he hadn't…"

"Then we would have ended up paying full price," Brady reassured her.

Silence fell between them. After a while,

Kelsey asked, "How'd you get to be so good at negotiating?"

Brady frowned. They were headed into dangerous territory again. "My dad was a notorious skinflint. He didn't pay one penny more than he had to for anything. I guess some of his frugality rubbed off." Brady paused, reflecting how little he still knew about big portions of Kelsey's life. He slanted her a curious glance. "What was your parents' attitude toward money?"

Kelsey rubbed the soles of her boots restlessly across the rubber floor mat. "Well, we never had enough of it, I can tell you that."

Brady had worried about a lot of things, growing up. Having enough money had not been an issue, however. He studied the brooding look on Kelsey's face. "And that experience has made you…?"

"Not want to count pennies," Kelsey said firmly, looking resentful again and staring straight ahead. "Not if I can help it."

They arrived at the auction barn and went inside. The tack from the big spread was in miserable condition overall. Kelsey took one look at it and was ready to forget it, but Brady was instantly intrigued. He fingered a bridle that was dirty and rough with age, seeing the possibilities, not just what was. "This stuff is awful," Kelsey said.

"Yeah, it is in deplorable condition," Brady agreed readily enough, going on to inspect a saddle that was in equally bad shape. He was getting excited despite the way Kelsey was turning up her nose. "But it's good-quality gear—some of the saddles in this group go for close to two thousand dollars each."

"When they're new and in good condition," Kelsey allowed.

Brady grinned and told her with a confidence he hoped would rub off on her, "These could be cleaned and treated with saddle dressing. A little elbow grease and they'll look like new. Same for the bridles, and the rest of the tack."

Kelsey still looked skeptical. "Half the buckles on this tack are broken, Brady."

Brady took her elbow and steered her over to a deserted corner of the auction house. He looked down at her, wondering how she could still manage to look so pretty and fresh when they'd been on the run all day. "A new buckle costs sixty-nine cents, and a solid brass alligator locking snap is six dollars. Compare that to a hundred dollars for each brand-new headstall, or a hundred-fifty for each brand-new breast collar—when between us we're going to have some forty horses to completely outfit—and you begin to see the wisdom of buying this in bulk at a greatly reduced price and repairing it. We can save literally thousands of dollars this way, Kelsey, and still have some darn fine gear for you and for me."

"Only one problem with your plan, Brady. I don't know how to repair tack." And, Brady could see, the thought of messing up some two thousand dollar saddle terrified her.

"It's not hard if you have the proper tools," he said amiably, reassuring her with a glance. "I'll teach you." It would be a good excuse to spend time together. A lot of time together. "Meanwhile," he continued amiably, "we ought to snap up that bin of horse blankets over there, too. A good washing and air-drying and they'll all be good as new."

"Okay," Kelsey sighed. "You've sold me." She looked deep into his eyes. "But you have to promise to help with all the extra work it entails."

Wishing he had the privacy to kiss her again, as thoroughly and completely as he wanted to kiss her at that moment, Brady put a hand across his chest. "Word of honor."

By the time they got back home it was nearly suppertime. Together, Brady and Kelsey carried the stacks of horse blankets and several piles of tack from the back of his pickup truck, into the barn. The rest of the saddles and the horses they'd bought would be delivered on Thursday. Then Brady went out to feed and care for the horses they did have. When he got back, he had hoped Kelsey would have washed up and started supper. He wanted to spend the evening together—and the time to do a little kissing, too.

Instead, the ranch house was empty. Her pickup truck was gone. On the coffee table in the living room she had left a note that read simply, "Back tomorrow. K. L."

Frowning, Brady looked around and found one other thing missing as well.

Chapter 6

Dani was cooking dinner with Beau when Kelsey rapped on their back door and walked in. "Sorry about my appearance," she said at her older sister's aghast look.

"What have you been doing?" Dani gave the chicken-and-rice dish another stir and set her spatula on the spoon rest. "You're covered in ranch dust from head to toe."

Kelsey washed her hands at the sink, then filched a slice of tomato from the salad Beau was making. "Brady and I bought some saddles and horses and stuff, and we carted some of it—like the horse blankets—home with us. They weren't washed yet and I got as much dirt on me as the back of his pickup truck."

"Where's Brady now?"

Kelsey paced the kitchen restlessly. "At the ranch, taking care of the horses and cattle we do have."

"Everything okay?" Dani asked.

"Yeah, sure," Kelsey fibbed, not about to tell her sister she didn't dare spend another night at the ranch alone with Brady, for fear of what she might want to happen, if she were left alone with him for too long. "It's just been a busy day." She didn't want to cap it off with another romantic rejection from Brady. "And I need to ask you a favor."

"Whatever we can do for you, we will," Beau said as he wrapped his arms around Dani's ever-expanding waist, and kissed her neck with husbandly affection. "You know that."

"Yeah." Kelsey tried not to notice how happy the two of them looked—how happy all her sisters looked, now that they were married to the men of their dreams. There was no reason for her to envy them. One day soon she would find her bliss, too. "Well, I just need to borrow a computer. Hopefully a laptop if you guys have a spare."

Beau frowned. "You're welcome to use mine, but it's over at my office on Main."

"I've got mine here. You can use that," Dani

said. She stood on tiptoe to kiss Beau's cheek and reluctantly extricated herself from his arms.

"Can I take it with me and bring it back to you tomorrow?" Kelsey said. "Maybe print some stuff then?"

"Absolutely. Whatever you need." Dani led the way to her study and packed it up for Kelsey in the carrying case.

"Well, I better get going," Kelsey said.

"And think about getting a shower while you're at it," Dani teased. "Or at least changing your clothes."

At the reference to her grubby state, Kelsey stuck out her tongue. Dani laughed. Both she and Beau waved as Kelsey drove off.

Instead of going home, Kelsey drove over to Jenna's apartment, parked behind the shop and, Dani's laptop in tow, headed up the stairs. Once inside, she stripped off her clothes and headed straight for the shower. Dani was right, Kelsey thought. She wouldn't feel great until she had washed off some of this grit.

Brady showered and shaved, and put on a clean set of clothes. Following his hunch about where his errant, unpredictable wife had gone, he drove into Laramie. Kelsey's pickup truck was right where he had expected it to be—parked behind

Jenna Remington's boutique on Main Street. He left his truck right behind hers, and took the exterior steps to the apartment two at a time. When she didn't answer his knock, he strode on in anyway and found Kelsey walking out of the bedroom. She was wearing one of the sexiest negligees he had ever seen. The powder-blue satin gown had a plunging back and pretty low front and was held up by a pair of very thin spaghetti straps. It clung to her curves like a second skin, clearly delineating breasts, waist, hips and thighs. Her long hair had just been washed and blow-dried—it tumbled softly to her shoulders. Her face looked freshly scrubbed, and the complete lack of artifice gave her an innocent look that was even sexier than the nightgown she wore.

Kelsey scowled at him. "I came over here to work," she said.

Brady grinned. She looked as ready to make love as he was to give it. "As what…?" he quipped. "A lady of the evening? Because if it's companionship you're looking for—" he tipped his hat at her and winked "—I volunteer."

"Very funny."

"It's no joke, Kelse." Brady took off his hat and set it on the table beside the door. He sauntered over to join her on the sofa. "I came to find you because I wanted to be with you tonight."

Kelsey did not look at him as she opened up the laptop computer on the coffee table and turned it on. "Well, I've got to work on my schedule of riding classes, and start pulling together some instructional packets for the students to take home. Rules of Riding Do's and Don'ts and things like that. I borrowed Dani's laptop computer and Jenna's apartment to do it, so if it's an evening of fun you're looking for, I suggest you go on down to Greta McCabe's dance hall and kick up your heels there."

"Without you? I don't think so. And that still doesn't explain the negligee you're wearing." He would've liked to think it was just for him, but since she clearly hadn't expected to see him tonight...

Kelsey sighed. "I left in such a hurry I forgot to bring any clothes with me. And this is the only kind of nightwear Jenna had in her closet. She's not exactly a T-shirt and jeans girl, you know, unless she's out at her and Jake's ranch. When she's in town, she's all sophistication. The only things in that closet are dresses and nightgowns like this."

"Well, you look...really nice...." Brady said at last, knowing that didn't begin to cover it. She looked sensational. He didn't know how he was going to get through the evening without making her his.

Kelsey gave him a brisk smile. "You look really nice, too, Brady." She pressed her lips together. Her shoulders drew tight as a bow as she focused on the laptop computer screen in front of her. "But that doesn't change the fact I've got work to do."

"Maybe I can help you," Brady offered.

Kelsey began to type with the hesitancy of a novice computer-user. "I don't think so."

"Okay, have it your way." Brady shrugged and headed for the refrigerator. They had all evening to get closer and figure out where this marriage of theirs was leading.

Kelsey sighed loudly as he opened the refrigerator door. "Now what are you doing?" she asked, clearly perturbed.

"Getting something to eat. I'm hungry." Brady hunkered down to survey the interior. He was not enthused about what he saw inside the refrigerator. "Unfortunately, there's not much in this refrigerator except diet soda and yogurt."

"Works for me just fine," Kelsey said. "But maybe you should hit one of the restaurants before you head back to the ranch." Not waiting for his reply, she began typing on the laptop computer again.

Brady watched her move the mouse with the same awkwardness she typed. At this rate, he thought, it was going to take her all night. Which maybe was the plan? "I could bring us something back, if you want."

"No, thanks. I'll be fine with the yogurt and diet soda."

Brady continued standing there. It didn't take a genius to see she had put him in the deep freeze. He had hoped this evening would be the start of their getting even closer. Instead, she looked like she couldn't be more miserable. "Did I do something wrong?" he asked, after a moment.

"No." Kelsey made a panicked face. "I did. Darn it, I can't get this graphics program to work!"

Glad they were now in an area he excelled in, Brady crossed to her side. He sat down beside her, so close their thighs were touching, and looked over her shoulder at the screen. "What are you trying to do?"

Kelsey lifted the laptop computer from the coffee table to her lap. "I wanted to make a big blue box, with red lettering inside it, but every time I attempt the red the blue goes away and now the darn thing has completely locked up." Kelsey tapped on the computer keyboard, trying several different things. She wiggled the red mouse key in the center of the keyboard. Nothing worked.

Brady leaned across her to see what he could do. "Let's use the escape key." Nothing. "Maybe this will work," he said, finally shifting the laptop onto his lap and taking over the keyboard. He typed in several variations and tried entering the commands into the computer. Still nothing.

As every effort to unfreeze the keyboard failed, Kelsey grew tenser and more worried. Finally, Brady sighed. "I think you've got a hardware problem here."

"You mean the computer is broken?"

"Yep, looks like. Because you can't exit any of the programs, and it won't even turn off."

Kelsey buried her head in her hands and looked all the more miserable. "Dani is going to kill me."

"It's not your fault," Brady soothed as he set the malfunctioning laptop on the coffee table once again.

"Well, it sure seems like it. The thing was fine when I picked it up." Kelsey gestured at it angrily. "I use it for half an hour, and now it's broken." She leapt up from the sofa and began to pace the small apartment.

Trying not to notice how the satin gown delineated Kelsey's ample curves, Brady returned his glance to her face. "We can get it repaired. She's probably got other computers at her house, right? Since she's a film critic and works at home?"

"Actually—" Kelsey bit her lip and swung back around to face Brady "—Dani's got several."

"Then it's no big deal." Brady shrugged. "I suppose, though, you and I should be getting a computer of our own. That way you could work at home." *And I wouldn't be chasing you all over Laramie County at night, just to spend time with you.*

Abruptly, the computer screen went blank. Noticing, Kelsey said, "Hey, it shut off all by itself."

But it didn't turn on again.

Nor, to Brady's disappointment, did Kelsey.

"You're really going to bed at eight-thirty at night?" he asked, when she had packed up her computer and the scribbled notes she had made.

Trying not to notice how he was looking at her—as if she were a forbidden dessert he would very much like to devour in one sitting—Kelsey smiled. "Yes. I'm very tired." She finished zipping up the carrying case, then straightened. "It's been a very long day. I just want to go to sleep." *Before I inadvertently screw up anything else. Like my "marriage."*

Brady shrugged, clearly disappointed. "Okay."

"So you can feel free to go home now," Kelsey continued, doing her best to get rid of him in as polite a manner as possible.

Brady stood and checked to see how much money was in his billfold. "I think I will go out and get some supper for us," he said.

Kelsey didn't like the possessive note in his low tone or the presumption in his eyes. That this was going to turn out to be some romance- or sex-filled evening after all. He had already turned her down twice. She wasn't giving him a chance to go all gallant on her and turn her down again. "I told you I'm not hungry."

"I'll bring it back. Just in case."

Kelsey rolled her eyes. She did not understand why this man would not give up on the idea of their spending the night together. It wasn't as if he had romance in mind, or would miss her if she weren't there. Besides, she needed time alone to collect her thoughts in a way that would prevent her from falling in love with someone who saw her only as a business partner and means to an end. "You're not sleeping in the same bed with me to-night," she warned him. Sleeping with him made her feel really married. And they weren't. Regardless of what Wade McCabe or her sisters thought. She needed to remember that before she found herself wanting to make love with him again.

Brady smiled at her matter-of-factly. "The sofa looks fine."

Kelsey tried not to think of the passionate kisses he had given her both times they had been in bed together. "There's a bed at the ranch," she said. It had been a little cramped and uncomfortable for two people who were trying to sleep without touching each other all night, but for one, it would do just fine.

Brady scowled and came closer. "If I sleep at the ranch tonight and you sleep here, as far as Wade McCabe and everyone else is concerned our marriage will be over, at least as far as appearances. Which would mean we'd be turning over the deed to the Lockhart-Anderson Ranch to him, pronto, and I'm not doing that. Hence, wherever you go, I go. Got it?"

Slowly, Kelsey let out the breath she had been holding. "Unfortunately."

"So back to dinner," he said. "Anything special you want?"

"No." She flashed him a tight, humorless smile. "Thanks."

"Okay." Brady grinned as if she had welcomed him warmly and shrugged. "I'll just wing it then." He grabbed his hat and put it on. "See you in a while."

Five minutes later, Brady walked into Callahan's Pizza and Subs. Mac Callahan, a stocky, friendly guy in his mid-twenties, was standing behind the counter. One of the young entrepreneurs in Laramie, he had opened his restaurant right out of college, and thanks to Mac's attention to quality and service, his business had been thriving ever since. "Hey, Mac," Brady said.

"Hey, Brady. Heard congratulations are in order."

"Thanks. Listen, you wouldn't happen to know how Kelsey likes her pizza, would you?"

Mac grinned the way everyone who knew they were newlyweds grinned. "Trying to surprise her with a honeymoon special, huh?"

Actually, Brady thought, he was trying to lure Kelsey out from behind a locked bedroom door. But that was another matter. One Mac didn't need to know about. "Here's hoping," Brady said casually, taking off his hat and hanging it on the rack next to the door. "So if you could help me out, I'd appreciate it."

"No problem." Mac picked up his order pad. "Kelsey's favorite is pepperoni, sausage and onions. Double cheese. Easy on the sauce."

"Sounds good to me. Make it an extra large. Add an order of buffalo wings, extra hot, and a hot Italian sub with everything in case she's of a mind to try that. We didn't have time to eat much today, we were so busy, so she's got to be as hungry as I am." For food, and other things as well…

While Mac began preparing the order, Brady leaned against the counter and watched. "You known Kelsey long?"

"I dated her. 'Course, near every guy in town can tell you that, too."

So Brady'd heard.

"She's a nice girl," Mac continued conversationally. "Hopelessly fickle, of course. Can't stay with anyone or anything for long." Mac slanted Brady a hope-filled glance. "Maybe that will change, now that she's got the ranch and you."

And maybe not, Brady thought, as he considered the way she was running hot and cold with him, recklessly inviting him into her bed one minute, kicking him out of it entirely the next. Hoping Mac's experiences with Kelsey could give him some insight into her behavior, Brady asked, "So how long did the two of you date?"

"Two weeks."

Brady warned himself not to jump to conclusions. "Did you dump her or did she dump you?" he asked casually.

Mac slid the pizza into the oven and started on the hot Italian sub. "That's not the way it works with Kelsey. She doesn't like ugly or emotional scenes. She just sort of eases away from a fella."

"Eases away," Brady repeated uncomfortably, not sure he understood.

"Well, starts losing interest," Mac explained further. "The signs are real subtle at first. She doesn't quite seem to be listening to what you're saying. Finds excuses to stay apart or spend time away from you. Before you know it, she's looking to somebody else." Mac snapped his fingers. "Then it's over. Just like that." Mac peered at Brady in concern. "Say, it's not happening to you already, is it?"

It better not, Brady thought grimly.

Kelsey was tossing and turning in bed, wishing she'd thought to smuggle in some of that yogurt for dinner before she had flounced off, locking the door behind her. Now it was too late, Kelsey thought as her stomach rumbled even louder. Because Brady was back. He was out in the living room. And worse, he had obviously brought food back with him, just as he promised. And not just any food. Mac Callahan's pizza.

Well, she had two choices. She could stay in here, pretending to be asleep, and starve to death. Or she could go out there and chow down. As always, the tomboy in Kelsey won out.

She threw back the covers and marched out into the living room to join Brady, hopelessly sexy negligee and all. He was sitting with his feet up on the coffee table, a plate of food in his lap, watching a popular sitcom.

Brady glanced over at her, taking in her tousled hair and irritated expression. For once, his eyes did not stray to her breasts. "That was quick," he said. "I haven't even had time to go to sleep yet and here you are already up, after a good…oh, thirty-five minutes' sleep."

Kelsey gave him a look that let him know she did not appreciate his attempt at humor at her expense. "Are you still sharing?" she demanded, getting right to the point.

Brady frowned as if that was a huge problem. "You told me you didn't want any dinner," he reminded her, squinting thoughtfully.

Her mouth was watering, her taste buds begging for even a smidgen of the food he'd brought back. "I changed my mind, okay?" Kelsey told him irritably, pushing the tousled hair off her face. "Now, can I have some or not?"

Brady flashed her one of his sexiest smiles. "Help yourself, darling. I figured you'd cave as soon as you smelled Mac's cooking—which I have to say is far superior to either yours or mine—so I got plenty."

She scowled at him—if this was his way of playing hard to get, and even harder to hold, it was working. Kelsey went to the kitchenette where he had left the food, and helped herself to a slice of pizza, a generous portion of wings and half the sub. She opened the fridge and found a six pack of cream soda. Regular, not diet. "You bought cream soda...."

"Mac Callahan said it was your favorite."

It was. Only problem, she could never remember to buy it when she was at the grocery store, and most vending machines didn't carry it, so she rarely had it. She paused to flip open the top and take a swig of the deliciously sweet soda. "You talked to him?"

"The whole time I was there," Brady affirmed in a smug know-it-all tone that had her alarm increasing by leaps and bounds.

Kelsey came over and sat down beside him on the sofa. "What did he say?"

Brady flashed her a wickedly mischievous grin. "Oh, lots of things. Most compelling were his tips on how to keep you interested in me." He winked. "Cream soda was right up there on the list."

Kelsey had a funny, sinking sensation inside her that for once had nothing to do with her desire for Brady. "You are joking, right?"

"Nope." Brady finished off one fiery-hot chicken wing and started on another. "Mac thinks, as does everyone else in town, that you are one fickle gal."

Kelsey broke off a chunk of pizza with her fingers. "That's just because we used to date and it didn't work out."

Brady narrowed his eyes at her. "It didn't work out with a lot of guys," he pointed out quietly.

Kelsey flushed. "Is that a criticism? Because, I'm telling you, Brady Anderson, if it is—"

He held up a staying hand before she could bolt to the relative safety of the breakfast room. "I'm just trying to understand you."

Kelsey blotted the corners of her lips with her napkin. "Not to mention how and why I got my reputation as a heartbreaker."

Brady shrugged, as if it didn't matter to him one way or another, when she could tell it did. "Well," he allowed, with a sexy wink, "now that you've brought it up, I wouldn't mind hearing your side of things."

To her surprise—usually she didn't give two figs what anyone thought of her—Kelsey wanted to confide in him. More than that, she wanted Brady to understand her the way no one ever had. "I have dated a lot of guys, but it wasn't because I wanted to set a record or anything. When I started out, I was just trying to find my own Mr. Right. And as soon as I realized the guy I was dating wasn't my Mr. Right, I ended it."

"Makes sense," Brady said, the gentleness in his eyes giving her the courage to go on.

"Usually someone else would ask me out straightaway, and I'd go, and then after a week or two, sometimes more, sometimes less, I'd find out he wasn't it for me, either," Kelsey said softly.

"And the more guys you rejected, the more of a challenge you became," Brady guessed.

Kelsey nodded, the bitterness and hurt she felt about that turn of events surfacing. "I sort of became the Mount Kilimanjaro of the fairer sex here in Laramie, and the guys around here began to want to go out with me, strictly for the challenge. It became a test of manliness, the quest to conquer me and take me to bed and steal my heart—and not necessarily in that order." She sighed, hating the way that had made her feel. She turned and looked deep into Brady's midnight-blue eyes. "That may not have been what they told themselves they were doing, you know. But it was what was happening nevertheless, and every time I realized I was just an object to be conquered, that rather than being themselves, the guys were doing everything and anything to please me, so they could go where no man had ever been before. Or worse, they were pretending to be something or someone they weren't, just so I'd think the two of us were a perfect match and I'd succumb to their charms. Each time, it was like a switch turned off inside me, and that was just it. It was over. I couldn't feel anything for them anymore, so then it was easier to break up with them."

Kelsey paused, hating the hopelessness she heard in her voice. She hadn't realized until now how much all the jockeying for her attentions had influenced her.

"Anyway, that's what I liked about you, Brady," she continued firmly, taking his hand in hers. "From the beginning there hasn't been any pretense. You are who you are, and that's that. There's no pretending anything with you. No ulterior reason on your part for being my friend and partner and now husband, and I appreciate that, more than you can know."

Abruptly, Brady looked uncomfortable. "I'm no saint, Kelse," he told her gruffly, extricating his hand from hers.

"But you're not using me," Kelsey persisted, letting him know with a look that he was different from all the other guys she had dated. "You haven't lied to me or pretended to be anything you're not, just so you could claim me and get me into your bed. The majority of those other guys did, whether they were conscious of it or not."

The way Brady looked at her then, as if there was nothing he wanted more than to make love to her, then and there, had Kelsey's pulse racing.

She swallowed. "Anyway, I think that's enough questions for one night," she said casually, putting her plate aside. "And I know I've had enough pizza." Enough rejection, in a sexual and romantic sense, too.

"Running out on me?" Brady said as they carried their plates to the kitchenette and set them there.

"Going to bed. Alone," Kelsey clarified, quickly putting the leftover food away, and letting him know with a look that despite how she was dressed there was not going to be any hanky-panky in that apartment that night.

Not just because they had nothing better to do. She had figured out the first time she had tried to go to bed with him, just for the heck of it, that she wasn't cut out for meaningless sex, even with someone as sexy and wonderful as Brady Anderson.

No, when she finally made love with a man it was going to have to be because she loved him, and he loved her, and for no other reason. She might be falling for Brady, big-time, but all he felt for her concerned business, with an occasional dash of lust and guilt, which wouldn't make for a satisfying sexual relationship, she was sure.

"Thanks for the dinner." She brought back a pillow and a blanket and set them down on the coffee table. Feeling reckless and mischievous again, she said, already backing toward her bedroom door, "Sweet dreams, cowboy. The sofa is all yours."

"And so is this," Brady said, taking her into his arms abruptly. Ignoring her soft gasp of surprise, he delivered a long breath-stealing kiss that had her middle fluttering weightlessly and her nipples aching. She surged against him, and he kissed her again and again, so thoroughly and completely that her knees went weak and she moaned her pleasure despite herself.

When he finally let her go there was no doubt he desired her. And intended to have her, as soon as the time was right. "Good night, Kelsey," he said.

"Good night."

Chapter 7

Kelsey's mood was blue the next morning as she took her clothes out of the compact washing machine in Jenna's apartment, and shook out the wrinkles as best she could. And it was bluer still after she'd gotten dressed and ready to go. "What's the matter?" Brady asked when she walked out into the kitchen to help herself to some of the coffee and blueberry muffins he'd brought back from Isabelle Buchanon's bakery down the street.

Kelsey sat down next to Brady at the small round table in the breakfast nook, between the kitchen and the living room. She spread her napkin across her lap, broke open her muffin and spread it with butter. Her expression still glum, she said, "I have to tell Dani I broke her laptop computer."

"You didn't break it," Brady corrected her, sipping his coffee. "It broke while you were using it. There's a difference, Kelse."

Kelsey warmed to the understanding she saw in his eyes, even though she knew it wasn't that simple. "Dani may not see it that way," she warned.

Brady frowned. His dark brows knit together in confusion. "Why wouldn't she?"

"Because—" Kelsey drew a long, steadying breath "—it wouldn't be the first thing of hers that I've borrowed and returned in less than stellar condition. One time I got barbecue sauce on a cashmere sweater. And then there was the blender that I borrowed for a party that didn't stand up to the amount of crushed ice I needed...."

"Even so, she's not going to be upset with you."

Kelsey sighed and gave Brady a skeptical look. She wished that were the case. But this computer had contained work Dani did for a living. Dani took her job as a movie reviewer very seriously, and so did Kelsey. If anything were to happen to any of Dani's work because of something Kelsey had done or not done, Kelsey would never forgive herself. Nor would Dani.

"Want me to go with you?" Brady asked. "I

was here. I saw what happened. I can talk to her about the problem."

Kelsey hesitated. She wasn't accustomed to leaning on anyone. Never mind a husband of her very own! But in this case, it would be good to have him by her side. Especially if things were as bad as she feared they would be. "If you wouldn't mind…" Kelsey said.

Brady shrugged his broad shoulders affably as he went over to rinse out his coffee cup and plate, and slid them into the dishwasher. "What are husbands for? Besides standing guard over you and sleeping on the sofa, that is."

Kelsey shot Brady a droll look and didn't respond to his teasing quip.

Looking determined to coax a smile out of her, no matter what it took, Brady put a hand to his spine and stooped over to walk like an eighty-year-old man with back trouble. "'Course, I may never walk straight again," he complained comically.

Truth to tell, Kelsey hadn't slept much better in the comfort of the bedroom, knowing he was in the next room, tossing and turning, just as she was. Trying not to think how sweetly and soundly she had slept when they'd been forced to share a mattress out at the ranch, she advised, "Next time aim for a bed."

"I will."

She caught her breath at the heat in his gaze. No doubt about what he was thinking there. No doubt about what she still wanted. Even if she'd come to her senses and realized it wasn't wise.

She had waited this long to make love with a man she loved. She could wait a little while longer for it to be right.

Why, then, did she keep wishing, deep inside, that it was him? Kelsey wondered. And why, then, did she keep wishing it would be soon?

"She's going to take the news about this well. You'll see," Brady continued encouragingly as he and Kelsey walked up to Dani and Beau's house and rang the bell shortly after breakfast.

Kelsey tucked her hand in his and held on to Brady as if it was the lifeline he was quickly turning out to be. She hoped he was right. She hated disappointing her sisters and/or being the cause of turmoil in the family. It was hard enough being the black sheep of the family.

Unfortunately, Brady was wrong about her sister taking the news well.

"You're sure it's broken?" Dani said, looking more panicked than she'd been about anything except her hasty marriage to Beau Chamberlain some months back. Of course she'd had good reason to be in a tizzy about that, Kelsey thought, since Dani hadn't initially believed she was married to Beau, never mind been able to remember the two of them saying "I do."

"Positive," Kelsey replied wearily. She leaned against a case of videotapes in Dani's home office, and folded her arms in front of her like a shield against the criticism sure to come.

"It completely froze up and then it went dead," Brady added.

"Let's just have a look," Beau said calmly, getting the laptop computer out of its case. He plugged it in and turned it on. As Kelsey had feared, absolutely nothing happened. No lights came on. No clicking or beeping sounds were heard.

"Oh, Beau, what am I going to do?" Dani asked as tears welled in her eyes. She sank into a chair and put her hands on her pregnant tummy. "I've got most of the book I've been writing on that computer's hard file!"

Kelsey had been afraid of that. "But you've backed them up on diskette, haven't you?" Beau said.

Tears fell down Dani's cheeks and splashed onto the desktop in front of her. "Not most of them. I meant to do it, but I just…"

Noting Brady looked confused, Kelsey turned to Brady and explained, "Dani's writing a book of film reviews for movies that are out on video."

"Months of work are on that computer!" Dani said, crying all the harder, making Kelsey feel worse.

"I'm sorry." Feeling as if she could not sink any lower, Kelsey burst into tears, too. "I'm really sorry." Unable to bear seeing her sister hurt any more, Kelsey spun around and ran out of the house to the pickup truck at the curb. She would have driven away, but she didn't have the keys. So instead she started walking blindly down the street, furiously blinking back a steady flow of new tears all the while.

She was halfway into the next block when a pickup pulled along beside her. Brady rolled down his window. He looked as calm as she was upset. "Kelsey, get in the truck," he said quietly.

Ignoring the compassionate gleam in his midnight-blue eyes, Kelsey shook her head and kept moving. She needed to be alone. She needed time to pull herself together. Couldn't he see that?

To her frustration, instead of heeding her request, Brady stopped the truck, got out and came marching down the sidewalk after her. Kelsey stiffened her spine, prepared to elbow him away from her. She wasn't prepared to have him drop down in front of her and circle an arm around her knees. Or pick her up and sling her over his shoulder, like a sack of feed.

Kelsey struggled to free herself and was rewarded with a tightened grip around her hips and thighs. She flailed her arms against his spine in a way that demanded he pay attention to her. "Brady Anderson, you put me down this instant!" she said as the ground swam before her eyes and she continued to look at the world upside down.

"Gladly." Brady continued striding along back to his truck. "As soon as I'm sure you'll listen to me."

Kelsey hated the smug male confidence in his low tone. Attitudes like that always brought out the worst in her, and this was no exception. "There's nothing to say," she countered rebelliously. As Kelsey struggled for balance, she put her hands around his waist.

Brady stopped beside the passenger door on his truck and set her down as abruptly as he had picked her up. He put his arms on either side of her, and using his torso, backed her up against the passenger door. "Sure there is," he said easily, looking down at her.

"No," Kelsey countered breathlessly, looking up into his dark blue eyes and wishing he would kiss her again, "there isn't."

He merely grinned and chucked her on the chin. "How about—" he paused to let his gaze rove her face, slowly and sensually "—we're going to Dallas, because I have a friend there who can repair any computer ever made?"

Even as she tingled at his nearness, Kelsey felt a brief ray of hope. It was quickly snuffed out by the reality of the situation. "Even if your friend can fix it, that may not help restore the data that was lost when it crashed," Kelsey answered him.

And if she had single-handedly destroyed, even inadvertently, months of her talented sister's work, Kelsey would know everything she and everyone else in the family had ever felt about her was true. It would mean she was and always would be a disaster waiting to happen.

"Well," Brady said, so gently it made her want to start crying all over again, "we'll never know until we try, will we?" He took her elbow and steered her aside, so he could open the passenger door for her. He brushed his lips against her temple. "Now, get in the truck so we can go."

An hour and a half later they were in the suburban home office of Maria Gonzalez. A pretty young woman with dark hair and even darker eyes, she led them into a well-equipped workroom containing computers of all shapes and sizes. Pictures of her family decorated the wall. As Kelsey looked at the photos of Maria and her clearly adoring husband and teenage daughters, she couldn't help but feel envious. What she wouldn't give for a little of this domestic bliss herself. Not that anyone needed to know that, of course, Kelsey thought. Because if they knew how much she wanted to love and be loved like that, they might start feeling sorry for her.

She'd had enough pity at the time her parents died to last a lifetime.

She didn't need any more.

"Thanks for fitting us in," Brady told Maria.

"No problem." Maria smiled. "You know I owe you. And Hargett, too. Without the two of you, none of this would be possible."

There was that name again, Kelsey thought.

And there was that look on Brady's face—the one that said he didn't want anything to do with Hargett.

It wasn't like him to be afraid of anything.

But, for some reason, he was afraid to have Kelsey learn much of anything about the rough-looking, very well-dressed man who had appeared, uninvited, at their ranch the day before.

Before Brady could stop her, Kelsey asked, "What exactly did Hargett and Brady do for you?"

Maria sighed as she set the laptop computer on her worktable and opened it. "I wanted to set this place up and work from home, but I couldn't get a loan from the usual channels. Brady heard about it and hooked me up with Hargett and I got as much money as I needed, right on the spot, no questions asked." She shrugged, allowing ruefully, "Of course the interest rate was a little higher than I would've paid at a bank, and the way Hargett kept checking in with me constantly to see how I was doing was a little—oh, unnerving—but I had so many referrals so quickly, I was able to pay the loan off within a year. And that was that."

Kelsey shot Brady a curious look. He gave her a look that said, "No more questions, Kelse." Then he stepped between her and Maria. "About this computer," Brady said firmly.

While Maria listened raptly, Brady explained how the laptop had frozen and then crashed.

Maria got out her tools and opened up the guts of the computer. The next hour and a half were devoted to a thorough check of the computer, and it was clear from Brady's constant involvement that he knew almost as much about how computers worked and stored information as Maria Gonzalez did.

Had it been Brady's hobby, Kelsey would not have been surprised. But he didn't even own a computer these days. Or if he did, she had never seen it.

So how, she wondered, had he gotten so knowledgeable?

Was this another part of his mysterious past?

The mysterious past that Hargett and now Maria were both connected to?

Kelsey understood Brady not wanting to talk about Hargett. Hargett seemed to make Brady very tense.

But she didn't understand him not wanting to talk about people like Maria. Maria was very nice, and still seemed to consider Brady her friend. Yet Brady had pretty much cut her out of his life, too. Why? Was it because of what Maria knew and accepted about Brady's connection to Hargett?

"It's a faulty switch," Maria explained to Kelsey, who was pretty much lost as to what the two were talking about, it was so technical. "All I have to do is replace it, and—" she finished putting it in "—voilà, power again."

Kelsey beamed. So far so good, then. "Can we tell if we lost any information when it crashed?" she asked nervously.

Maria nodded. "I'll let you know as soon as I finish checking the hard drive."

While Kelsey paced the workroom, and Brady watched over Maria's shoulder, Maria typed in a lot of complicated commands.

"Apparently, all you lost was whatever you were working on yesterday after 5:00 p.m.," Maria told Kelsey seriously, "because until then, the records show all the information entered into the computer was saved and is still in good shape."

Kelsey breathed a sigh of relief. "Then it's just my stuff that was lost, and that was not important." She felt like dancing a jig.

"Thanks a lot, Maria. We really appreciate this," Brady said as he pulled out his wallet.

Maria stopped him from paying her. "I owe you, Brady. Big-time. I'm just glad I got to see you again. I thought—when you and Hargett had that big falling-out—I might never see you again."

Briefly, sorrow creased Brady's handsome face. "I'm sorry I haven't been in touch," he said as he put his wallet back in his pocket.

"Well, don't let it keep happening," Maria scolded warmly. "I want you—and Kelsey here—to come over and have dinner with the whole family soon."

Again, that reluctant look on Brady's face. "We'll try," he said.

"Do better than that. Do it. And by the way—" Maria glanced at the wedding rings both were wearing "—isn't there a little something else you neglected to tell me?" she teased. "Like just how long the two of you have been married?"

Brady grimaced. "Three days."

Maria's eyes widened. "What about your honeymoon?" she asked, aghast.

"Long story," Brady said.

"And then some," Kelsey agreed, figuring there was no need to get into all that now.

"Hmm." Maria studied them both, this time seeing a lot more than Kelsey would have liked. "Well, I'm just glad you got married, Brady," Maria murmured, after a moment. Her dark eyes softened sympathetically. "Given the way you felt after your break-up with Rexanne—"

"Water under the bridge," Brady interrupted.

"Yeah." Maria got his hint, loud and clear, and did not continue with whatever it was she was about to say. "I guess it is."

Chapter 8

"So who was Rexanne and when were you engaged to her?" Kelsey asked curiously the moment the two of them got into Brady's pickup truck to head back to Laramie.

Brady kept his eyes on the road. "It was a couple years ago," he divulged in a way that let Kelsey know he would appreciate it if she didn't ask any more questions. "And she was just somebody I worked with."

Kelsey knew she would never understand Brady unless she understood whatever it was that had made him run from his old life. She wanted to understand him. Not just as his "temporary wife," but as his friend and his partner. She studied his handsome profile and the brooding look in his midnight-blue eyes.

"Did she cheat on you?"

For a long moment, Brady was silent. "It's a lot more complicated than that."

Kelsey waited, hoping he would explain. Finally, he did. "Rexanne was very pretty and very sought after. She'd had dozens of boyfriends, and even several failed engagements before I met her, and as much as I hate to admit it, I think that was even part of the attraction between us."

"Sort of like the guys I've been dating," Kelsey interrupted.

Brady nodded. "Right." A remoteness she hadn't heard before crept into his tone, as he continued self-effacingly, "I liked the challenge of making a woman like that mine. And up until then I'd been pretty restless. Dating a lot of women. Hoping to find The One, but finding none of them interesting enough to hold my attention long-term."

Kelsey understood that. She had done her share of fruitless searching, too. She knew what it felt like to constantly have everything turn out wrong. It was very frustrating and disappointing, to say the least. "But Rexanne did keep your interest," she surmised.

"Looking back, I think it was more the challenge of making her mine than anything else. She had such a reputation for being unattainable."

Kelsey tensed, uncomfortably aware of how the two situations mirrored each other. "Rexanne played hard to get?" Kelsey guessed, aware she was beginning to feel just a tad bit jealous for the first time in her life. Usually, she didn't care who the other women had been in her boyfriend's life.

Brady nodded. "Oh, yeah. She made me work for that first date, and every one after that. And I'd be lying if I said I didn't find that exciting at the time, 'cause I did." He paused to shoot Kelsey a brief, honest look before returning his attention to the road. "Here, I had all these other women lined up, wanting to marry me. Whereas Rexanne wouldn't give me the time of day."

"But she did finally agree."

"Yep." Brady turned on his left signal. As soon as it was clear, he guided the pickup into the far left lane of the freeway. "And that's when the problems started on my end," he admitted as he accelerated to keep up with the fast-flowing traffic. "I felt so trapped. Restless. I guess deep down I knew I didn't love her, not the way I should, not enough to make a marriage last, but I'd made this commitment to her. I didn't think I could or should back out."

Brady paused and shrugged his broad shoulders affably. "Anyway, the wedding plans continued full steam ahead all the way till the week of the wedding. And that was when I began to get the feeling something was wrong on her part, too."

He sighed unhappily as he continued to recollect. "Rexanne denied it, of course. She was determined not to let her family down again, determined to prove she could remain faithfully devoted to just one man. And I know she didn't want to hurt me. But my uneasiness persisted, and the night of the wedding rehearsal I caught this glimpse of her looking at Zeke, my best man, and him looking at her, and there was such longing there, such connection, I knew—even though neither of them had done anything about it—that she'd fallen in love with Zeke. So I confronted them, and they admitted it was true, and we called off the wedding that very evening to the great disappointment of family and friends. And Rexanne married Zeke the next day—in my stead."

Kelsey stared at him, unable to believe he was so matter-of-fact about it all, after suffering what had to have been a major humiliation, being left at the altar that way. Her heart going out to him, she asked softly, "Is that when you sort of dropped out of sight?"

Just that quickly, the expression on Brady's face

closed down. "Let's just say the whole experience made me seriously reevaluate my life," he said carefully after a moment. Seeing their exit coming up, he turned on his right signal, checked to make sure it was clear, and began getting over into the far right lane. "I knew I wasn't happy." His lips pressed together as he steered the pickup down the exit ramp. "I'd been counting on my marriage to Rexanne, the acquisition of a wife and kids and a satisfying family life of my own, to make me happy. But in retrospect, I realized the vague sense of dissatisfaction I had was more deeply rooted than that," he told her seriously. As they stopped at a traffic light at the bottom of the ramp, he turned to face Kelsey. "I needed to do some soul-searching of my own and figure out where I belonged, what kind of life I wanted, before I made a commitment like that to anyone else."

Kelsey searched his eyes. "Are you happy now?"

"With ranching? Yeah." Brady smiled, and the joy he expressed then seemed to radiate from deep inside his heart. "Happier than I've ever been in my life."

When the light changed, Brady drove a quarter mile down the road and pulled into the gas station on their right. "Do you still want a wife and kids?" Kelsey asked as he parked in front of the pump and cut the motor.

"I've got a wife, remember?" Brady took her hand in his and lifted it to his lips. He pressed a tender kiss into her palm. He shot her an intent look that took her breath away before continuing, just as contentedly, "And I wouldn't mind a few kids."

Kelsey blushed and tried not to think about how those kids he wanted would likely be made. Knowing Brady, it wouldn't be in some test tube or medical lab. She swallowed hard and tugged her hand away from his. Blushing, she grabbed her purse, got out of the truck and walked around to where the gas gauge was. "Let's not put the cart before the horse, okay?" She slid her credit card into the slot on the pump that allowed them to pay for their purchase outside.

Brady laced his arm around her shoulders and leaned down to whisper in her ear. "We could always adopt if you don't want to do it the old-fashioned way," he teased.

Kelsey's flush deepened, despite her efforts to remain cool, calm and collected. That was the problem, if she ever had children with Brady, she did want to do it the old-fashioned way. And judging from the look on his face, he knew it, too.

Unfortunately, they couldn't do that unless, or

until, they had a real marriage, and right now they were far from that. They hadn't slept together. And they certainly hadn't mentioned being in love with each other. Although, she was beginning to think, on her part, that was exactly what was happening....

Determined to change the subject, to something even more important to her and less comfortable for Brady this time, she said, "Were you working for this guy, Hargett, when all this happened?"

Brady's expression shifted from good to bad, just as she had suspected it would. Clearly, this subject was not welcome. He dropped his hold on her, punched a couple of buttons on the pump. "Yes," he said abruptly, the look he gave her, as he opened the fuel door and took off the gas cap, forbidding her to ask anything more.

Kelsey paused, wondering what the source of the tension between Brady and Hargett was.

Knowing there was only one way to find out, she ignored Brady's warning look and asked idly, anyway, "Hargett doesn't happen to own a savings and loan, does he?"

Brady shot her a look as if wondering where on earth she had gotten that idea. "No," he said flatly. "He's an independent businessman."

An independent businessman. That could mean anything—and not necessarily good, either.

"What does he sell?" Kelsey asked, her sense that Brady was deliberately shielding her from something unpleasant or shameful stronger than ever.

Brady shot her a sharp look that seemed resentful of her nosiness. "Why does it matter?"

Because, Kelsey thought to herself, *whatever is going on between you and Hargett is wedging a distance between you and me.* But wary of revealing the extent of her feelings to Brady, lest she ruin their partnership because he didn't feel anywhere near the same way about her, Kelsey fell silent.

She thought a moment more, about the rough-hewn man in the expensive suit. He loaned out money at higher than usual interest rates, to people like Maria who couldn't otherwise get a loan for what they wanted to do, and then came around and checked on them to the point it was unnerving to them.

She knew of only one job that fit that description.

She watched as Brady replaced the nozzle on the pump and screwed the gas cap back on. "Is he a loan shark then?"

Brady burst out laughing, as if the whole idea were absurd. "I never thought of it that way," he answered finally, still grinning at what was apparently an insider's joke.

And to Kelsey's frustration, that was all he would say on the subject, even after they'd taken their credit card receipt from the slot and had gotten back on the highway home.

They stopped en route to Laramie to see a bull and some Black Angus cows Brady was interested in. With the last of the money Wade McCabe had loaned them, Brady negotiated a pretty savvy deal for both cattle and bull. All would be delivered to their ranch the following day.

"You know, you'd be a pretty good businessman," Kelsey said, unable to help but be impressed, although she was still a little ticked off he wouldn't tell her more about this mysterious Hargett. But that was Brady. He was always playing his cards close to his vest. She just wished his secretiveness about his past life wasn't beginning to hurt so much. She wanted him to trust her enough to be able to tell her anything and everything. Because without that kind of intimacy, there could be no real and lasting love between them, that much she knew.

Brady drew up alongside the mailbox. The red flag was down, so that meant the postman had already come. "A rancher is a businessman, Kelse."

Kelsey leaned out across the open truck window and got the mail out of the black metal mailbox and their afternoon newspaper out of the newspaper carrier underneath the box. "You know what I mean," she said as she set it all on her lap then rifled through a stack of mostly bills and a few catalogs. It was all for her. Brady had his delivered to a post office box in town.

"Yeah, I do." Brady turned his truck into their gravel lane, kicking up clouds of dust behind them. "And the range is the only place I want to be," he said, staring straight ahead, both hands clenching the wheel. "So forget trying to make me into the next Texas billionaire."

Kelsey caught the edge in his voice as he whipped the pickup around to a rather fancy stop, next to one of the barns. It was the first time Brady'd been really short with her in the five months they'd known each other. Which told her just how close to the bone she'd cut.

"Sorry," she said after a moment. "I didn't mean to get under your skin." She hopped down from the truck and circled around the back. Together, they stood there, admiring the crisp fall weather and the blue Texas skies overhead. It was close to seventy degrees. A light breeze ruffled the turning leaves on the trees. Kelsey looked down at the scuffed toes of her boots. "I know how it is to have people wishing you were something you aren't," she told him. And it hurt, no two ways about it.

Brady took her elbow with one hand, and carried Dani's repaired laptop computer in his other as he steered her toward the back stoop. "You talking about your sisters?"

Kelsey shrugged, pretending as if it didn't matter to her in the least. "Everybody who knows me, actually," she said as Brady unlocked the door and ushered her inside the mud room, and from there into the ranch house kitchen. "Everybody had an idea what I should be. Secretary, flight attendant, saleswoman—you name it, I've not only been pushed to those jobs, I've held them."

Brady set the laptop on the table, then took two soft drinks out of the refrigerator. The house was a little stuffy after being closed up all day, Kelsey noted. She watched as Brady went over to open up the window above the kitchen sink.

"Twenty-four jobs in six years, isn't it?"

Kelsey tilted her head to study him better as she leaned against the opposite counter, wary of getting overly comfortable with him. "How'd you know that?" Now that she was on the receiving end of the nosy questions, she found to her surprise she wasn't any happier about them than he had been.

Brady's lips tipped up ruefully at the corners. "Let's just say I was warned not to get involved in any kind of partnership with you, by just about everyone," he said.

Kelsey found herself bristling at the implied criticism of her past. She regarded him steadily over the rim of her soft drink can. "Why did you, then?"

"I don't know exactly," Brady said, shrugging as if some things weren't meant to be looked at too closely. "It was just something I wanted to do," he explained.

Kelsey nodded and turned her glance away. She couldn't help but wish he had given her a more poetic reason for the two of them being together, instead of just out-and-out gut instinct and stubbornness, but at least he was honest about what he was feeling.

That counted for a lot.

She couldn't imagine being involved with someone who wasn't honest with her.

Because without truth, what was there?

Brady frowned as he looked at the feed store calendar hanging on the wall. "I can't believe the week is half over," he said, shaking his head. "Wednesday night already!"

Wednesday night!

Oh, no, Kelsey thought. Quickly, she glanced at Brady's watch. "What time is it?" she said anxiously.

"A little after six, why?"

Because she had a date with Rafe Marshall tonight, that was why! Figuring however, that Brady might not cotton to that idea, given the way it might appear to others, she decided to spare him any worry as she took a big gulp of her drink and then tightened her fingers around the can. "No problem, really. I just have to be somewhere at seven."

He scanned her from head to toe, taking in her red chambray shirt, jeans, hat and red cowgirl boots. "You want me to go with you?" he asked cheerfully.

Kelsey wished he could, but in this case, three really would be a crowd. "Nope," she shot back, just as agreeably. "Just stay here, take care of the ranch, and get ready for all the horses, cattle and tack we're having delivered tomorrow." Thursday looked like it was going to be a good day. And once it was over, they would have everything they needed to turn this homestead from an iffy operation to a first-rate spread.

Brady stepped close enough for her to take in the tantalizing masculine fragrance of his skin and hair and the warmth of his body. Was it her imagination or did he have loving her on his mind?

"You going to be here for dinner?" he asked, running a hand lightly down her arm, eliciting delicious tingles everywhere he touched and some places he didn't, as well.

I'd sure as shootin' like to be, Kelsey thought, *given the sexy new light in your eyes.*

As she tried to figure out how to handle this very tricky situation, Kelsey made a vague, noncommittal sound in the back of her throat.

She really didn't want to hurt Brady's feelings by shutting him out this way, but Rafe Marshall had sworn her to secrecy, and a promise was a promise.

"Um, no." Now that she was the one deliberately shutting him out of a part of her life, she found she couldn't quite meet his eyes.

The heat of a self-conscious flush in her cheeks, she made a big show of sorting her mail and stacking it neatly in the letters rack beside the kitchen telephone.

"Listen, would you mind taking the computer back to Dani?" Kelsey said as she grabbed her catalogs and put them on the bookshelf where the cookbooks should have gone, if she'd had any. She turned and looked at Brady directly. "I know we were going to do that together this evening, but now I really don't have time," she said honestly.

"No problem," Brady said with an affable shrug.

"Thanks." Ignoring the mounting curiosity on Brady's face, Kelsey rushed up the stairs to get ready for her secret date.

Chapter 9

She was not cheating on him, Brady told himself firmly, the entire time he was outside taking care of the horses. And there was no reason to think that might be so. Kelsey wasn't even all that interested in having a fling with him. She hadn't had the time or the inclination to go after another man. Besides, they were married. The deed to her beloved family ranch was on the line. She wouldn't do anything to screw that up.

But when he saw her run out of the house in a dress and high heels, looking pretty enough to pose for wedding pictures, he was no longer sure of anything.

His options were limited. He could deliver Dani's computer to her, and then return home and sit here at the ranch and wait for Kelsey to come back. Or he could follow her and find out what she was up to tonight. Even before he emerged from the barn, Brady knew what he was going to do.

For a while, as the two of them drove the country roads, Brady was worried Kelsey might realize he was behind her. But she didn't. And when she turned into the Gilded Lily and parked in front of the nicest restaurant in a thirty-mile radius and was helped out of her car by none other than a dark-haired man in a suit and tie, he understood why she had dressed up so much.

She was having a secret rendezvous!

Teeth gritted, Brady watched as his wife was escorted into the restaurant by her "date." When they had disappeared inside, he guided his truck all the way into the parking lot. He didn't know why he was so hurt. It wasn't as if he and Kelsey were really man and wife. Brady just knew that he was hurt. But maybe that was his fault, too, he conceded. For not following through on what she had obviously wanted and making her his woman as well as his wife from the beginning.

The question was, was it too late to go back and do what he should have done on the very day they married?

* * *

"You've got to relax, Rafe." Kelsey smiled as he helped her into her seat.

"Sorry. I'm just so rusty at all this. I feel like I'm all thumbs."

"Patricia is not going to mind if you eat your salad with your dinner fork and your dinner with your salad fork, or forget to put your napkin on your lap before your first sip of water."

"But she will mind if I do something stupid like close her dress in the door," Rafe said.

"I think you should just be yourself," Kelsey soothed. Seeing how nervous Rafe still was, she reached over and took his hand in hers. "Honestly," she said, staring deep into his eyes with as much confidence-inspiring intensity as she could, "everything is going to be fine. You'll see."

At the door there was a commotion. A shadow fell over them. Kelsey looked up to see Brady glaring at both of them. "So this is what you're up to tonight," he said grimly.

"It's not what it looks like," Kelsey said quickly, standing, too.

"Oh, isn't it?" Brady volleyed back. He crossed his arms in front of him and his jaw hardened all the more.

"No," Kelsey spelled out, just as plainly as her heart took on a rapid, thudding beat. "It is not."

She propped her hands on her hips and gave Brady a stern look. "And if you'll calm down, and sit down, Rafe and I will explain."

To Kelsey's chagrin, Brady's blue eyes turned even stormier. Up till now, Brady had always been so easygoing, even in the tensest situations. She hadn't figured he had a jealous bone in his body. That showed how much she knew!

"The only explanation I want to hear from you is going to be at home," Brady told her in a low tone that brooked no arguments. Brady took her by the elbow.

Kelsey shook off his grip and tilted her chin at him. "I'm not leaving here, Brady. Rafe and I have a date tonight—"

Looking as if he had just been pushed to the absolute limit, Brady stared at her. "And you see nothing wrong with dating him while you're married to me?" he queried coolly.

Given the fact they had yet to exchange anything except a few heated kisses and a lot of empty promises? "As it happens, no, I don't."

Sensing trouble, Rafe stood, too.

His nervousness of just moments before gone, he looked at Brady like the calm, personable elementary school principal he was. "Brady, I think you should listen to her," Rafe advised quietly.

"Oh, you do, do you?" Brady countered sarcastically as heads turned all around them, and all other conversation in the room ground to a halt as the diners gawked at the three of them.

"Yes," Rafe replied urgently, on Kelsey's behalf, beginning to sweat. "It's all perfectly innocent."

Brady shook his head and continued to look as if he longed to punch something.

"If you think that, you're as messed up as she is…." Brady swore at Rafe in a low, furious voice.

The maître d' hovered behind them, like the referee in a boxing ring. "Please, folks. No scenes."

Brady turned around grimly. "Don't worry. There isn't going to be one," he told the maître d'. "I've seen all I need to see." Ignoring Kelsey altogether, he turned on his heel and walked out of the restaurant.

"You need to go after him," Rafe whispered as soon as Brady had bolted out the door.

Kelsey sat down at the table. She was so embarrassed her face felt as if it were on fire. She had always hated it when people underestimated her, or thought the worst of her, without first taking the time to try to understand what was going on with her. Her sisters had been doing it for years. When they weren't jumping to conclusions, they were assuming she would fail at whatever she attempted. Only Brady had been different.

From the very moment they met, he had ignored what everyone else said about her, or thought about her, and accepted her for what and who she was. That was one of the reasons she had found herself willing to form a partnership with him, and also why she had begun falling in love with him.

But now he was like everyone else.

Automatically thinking the very worst of her.

And it hurt. A lot.

But maybe that was what she got, Kelsey thought, for opening up her heart to him, and making herself vulnerable.

Well, no more.

He was either going to have to clean up his act and go back to trusting her again or go back to wherever it was he had come from. And she was going to tell him that as soon as she caught up with him again.

Meanwhile, she had a vow of her own to keep. She looked at Rafe and smiled. "I promised you I would help you get over your jitters and I will. Now, let's just sit here and have dinner and a nice conversation and I'll tell you if I see any red flags about the way you intend to carry out your date with Patricia...."

As Kelsey had suspected, Rafe was not nearly as rusty as he thought.

He forgot to ask her if she wanted dessert before he consulted with the waiter, and he stepped on her toes several times when they were dancing after dinner, but all in all, he was fine. And a lot more confident at the end of their two-hour date than at the beginning of it. The two of them said good-night, and then, her stomach in knots as she thought about seeing Brady again, and probably continuing the fight that they had started but not really finished in the restaurant, Kelsey drove back to the ranch.

Brady's truck was out front, but the ranch house was dark and silent. She went inside, wondering if he was already in bed for the night, even though it was barely ten o'clock, but he was nowhere to be found.

She went out to the barns and looked around. He wasn't there, either.

Kelsey went back to the house and sat down to wait.

One hour passed, then another. Finally, around midnight, she heard the sound of an approaching rider on horseback. She looked out and saw Brady ride into the yard next to the stables. He swung down off the horse, and then proceeded to take off the saddle and rub down the animal, before turning him out to pasture for the night with the other horses on the ranch.

His strides heavy but purposeful, he disappeared into the stable with the rest of the tack. Another five, ten, fifteen minutes passed and he still didn't emerge.

Tired of waiting for him, Kelsey walked out to the stables. She heard the sound of water running as soon as she was inside the cement-floored building with the wooden stalls.

She headed down to the stable manager's office. Brady had turned it into his private quarters when he moved out to the ranch. There was still a desk and file cabinets there, but he had pushed those to one side of the room. The other side of the small room held an old-fashioned iron cot, made up with white sheets and green wool blankets. The original bathroom with sink and commode had been left intact, but Brady had put in the kind of utilitarian metal-walled shower stall they used in high school locker rooms beside that.

He was currently in the shower. He had obviously stripped off his clothes the moment he walked in—they were hanging over the sides of the stall. Kelsey thought about backing out of the room, then decided against it.

They were married.

And she'd already seen him naked.

She could handle this. His intimate parts were shielded from view. All she could see from her vantage point were his legs, from his calves on down, and his head and shoulders above the metal sides.

He turned to glare at her as she came in, then, his mouth clamped shut furiously, finished shampooing his hair in utter silence. He ducked his head under the stream, rinsed off, and then shut off the water.

The silence that followed was broken only by the sounds of the water running down the drain next to his bare feet.

Her heart pounding at the showdown to come, Kelsey stayed where she was until he emerged from the shower stall, dark blue towel slung low across his hips, in a way that made his broad shoulders and muscled chest look even sexier and more buff. With difficulty, Kelsey tore her eyes from his slicked-back hair and damp skin. "What do you want?" he said.

"Exactly what you'd think," Kelsey replied, mocking his sarcastic tone to a T. "To talk to you."

He quirked a discerning brow. "Without your boyfriend?"

Kelsey's temper flared. There was nothing she hated more than having those close to her simply suppose the worst about her, instead of taking the time to understand. She smiled at Brady tightly and moved away from the wall. "Rafe is not my boyfriend."

Brady shrugged and went over to the sink. He lathered up his face and began to shave. "Could have fooled me and everyone else in that restaurant." He looked at her in the mirror. "Or do you hold every guy's hand like that?"

Determined to set the record straight, Kelsey moved closer yet. She continued to hold Brady's eyes in the mirror while he shaved with quick, precise strokes of the blade. "I was doing him a favor."

Brady finished and rinsed his jaw. He patted his face dry with a hand towel, then said in a low, bored tone, "Maybe you really shouldn't tell me any more."

Clamping her lips together in frustration, Kelsey stalked even closer. "It was a pretend date, Brady."

"Well, that's a new one," Brady drawled as he slapped on a generous amount of wintry-smelling aftershave.

Ignoring his sarcasm, Kelsey propped both her hands on her hips and continued explaining her actions in the most matter-of-fact tone she could manage. "Rafe wants to ask Patricia Weatherby out and he came to me for help. He thought if he had a trial run of the evening he planned for himself and Patricia, the real date with Patricia would go a lot more smoothly. All I was doing tonight was giving him dating tips. There was nothing of a romantic nature going on."

Finished, Brady turned to face her and leaned against the sink. His glance roved her mocha-brown stretch-velvet dress, taking in the way the fabric molded snugly to her every curve before swirling prettily to mid-calf.

"Yet you stayed at the restaurant with him," Brady said, his eyes roving the high neck and fitted long sleeves, before returning to her face. "Instead of coming home with me."

Kelsey shrugged and paced the room restlessly, her high heels clicking against the cement floor. She knew what Brady wanted, but she refused to apologize for not giving in to Brady's husbandly demands. "He's a friend and I had promised to help him," she said. As far as she was concerned, that should be explanation enough.

"Yeah, well—" Brady leaned closer as she strode past. He caught her arm and swung her around to face him. *"I'm your husband."*

"In name only," Kelsey corrected him icily, still seeing red over the way he was behaving, as she pried his fingers from her upper arm. "And where do you get off acting so possessive, anyway?" she demanded indignantly. "It's not as if we're really man and wife."

Brady's brow lifted in a manner that was all the more possessive. He backed her up against the wall, so his hips pressed into hers. "Well, maybe we should be," he said.

"What's that supposed to mean?"

Brady leaned in even closer. He let his towel drop to the floor and his hands came up to cup her shoulders. "What do you think it means?"

Engulfing her with the heat and strength of his body, he lowered his head and delivered a breath-stealing kiss. She moaned, and he kissed her again, shattering what little caution she had left. Her lips parted beneath the pressure of his as his tongue swept her mouth with long, sensuous strokes. He encircled her with his heat and strength until Kelsey's whole body was alive, quivering with urgent sensations unlike any she had ever felt.

"Brady—" Kelsey moaned again as his hands swept down her body, molding and exploring through the soft, stretchy fabric of her dress. It felt so good to be wanted and touched. It felt so good to be held against him like this. To have the barriers between them start coming down. Desire trembled inside her, making her tummy feel weightless, soft. She melted helplessly against him, thigh to thigh, sex to sex. She could feel his erection pressing against her, hot and urgent, his heart pounding in his chest.

"I'm through pretending I don't feel the way I feel. I want you, Kelsey," he whispered, raining kisses down her throat, across her cheek, her lips. Framing her face with his hands, he forced her mouth up to his. "I want you to be mine." He tunneled his hands through her hair, tilted her head back and kissed her with surprising tenderness. Lifting his head from hers, he asked in a low voice that seemed wrenched from his very heart, "What do you want?"

He was so strong and wonderful. He tasted so good, so undeniably male, so right. "You," she whispered, her hips moving against his as he continued to watch her in that unsettling way. "I want you...."

"No more holding back, then," he promised her softly. "This time we're really going to do this."

"Yes," Kelsey said, quivering at the tightening of his muscles beneath her fingertips and the heat flowing into his bare skin. She had never experienced anything like this intense, aching need. She didn't care if she was behaving recklessly once again. She wanted to see where the passion would lead them. Would it bring her as close as she wanted to be to Brady? Would making love link them forever, make them truly man and wife?

His legs pinning hers to the wall, he bent his head and kissed her with a passion so hot it sizzled. His tongue flicked across the edges of her teeth, before delving deep in a slow mating dance. Joy swept through her and Brady's hands moved behind her. The zipper of her dress slid down. The next thing she knew, he was pushing it off her shoulders, letting it fall to the floor. His whole body was quaking as he regarded her transparent black lace bra, thigh-high stockings and damp bikini panties. "You are so beautiful. So sexy," he murmured, and then those came off, too.

Wanting to remember everything about this night, Brady let his glance sift slowly over her. Kelsey was gorgeous, no matter what she was wearing. But she had never looked more radiant than she did at that moment, with color blushing her freckled cheeks, and her cinnamon-red hair tumbling over her pale shoulders.

His gaze moved over her supple curves, her long slender legs and silky thighs, the shadowy vee. He knew they were far from solving all their problems, but he didn't care. He couldn't wait any longer. He had to make her his.

She trembled as he bent and kissed her ripe coral nipples one by one. She clasped his shoulders and sagged against the wall as his mouth moved urgently on her breasts. He slid down her body, kissing the hollow of her stomach, stroking the soft insides of her thighs. He traced her navel with his tongue, then dropped lower still, to deliver the most intimate of kisses, until she was awash in pleasure, shuddering.

Achingly aware of every soft warm inch of her, Brady laid her down on the cot and stretched out over top of her. Savoring the sweetness of her unexpected acquiescence to him, he closed his eyes, lowered his mouth to hers and let her lead him where she wanted to go. He groaned as their tongues twined urgently and his body took up a primitive rhythm all its own, until there was no doubting how much they needed each other, needed this. And then she was lifting her hips, pleading wordlessly for a more intimate union. He edged her knees apart, lifted her up and eased into her, past that first fragile barrier, not wanting to hurt her for anything. Her eyes widened in surprise, in pain, even as her body stretched to take him.

"That's it, sweetheart," he whispered, deepening his penetration even more as he kissed her slowly, thoroughly. "Take all of me."

Kelsey didn't think it was possible. He was so big, so hard. She was so tight. But as he slid one arm beneath her and arched his body up and all the way into hers, she found it was possible after all. Not only possible, but wonderfully sensual, hot and wild. Loving the tender but fierce way he was possessing her, she closed her eyes, awash in sensation. Brady kissed her again, his body taking up the same slow, timeless rhythm as his tongue. And then she was moaning again, moving against him, with him, able to hear the soft, whimpering sounds in the back of her throat, and the lower, fiercer sounds in his. What few boundaries that still existed between them dissolved. She ran her arms along his arms, across his shoulders, down his back. Their spirits soared as he pressed into her as deeply as he could go, withdrew, then filled her again. And they were lost in the ecstasy, free-falling into pleasure unlike anything Kelsey had ever known.

Long moments passed as they clung to each other, still trembling, still in awe at what they'd done. Finally, Brady rolled onto his back. Kelsey had only to look at his face to see his regret. "It shouldn't have happened like that."

She rolled onto her side, disappointed he didn't look as happy about what had just happened as she was. She had thought this would change everything. Apparently not. At least not in the way that she had hoped.

She felt her defenses go back up, as surely and swiftly as they had come down. "What do you mean?" she asked warily, doing her best to hide her hurt that he could find anything wrong with what had just happened between them.

Brady turned troubled eyes to hers. "Here," he told her, not bothering to mask his guilt. "On a cot in the stable. In the midst of an argument. You are—were—a virgin, for heaven's sake. Not to mention, my wife. At the very least, it should have been in a real bed," he said thickly. "With candles and roses all around. Maybe even some champagne and strawberries or something."

The source of his worry identified, Kelsey smiled and began to relax. Brady's concern for her was sweet but hopelessly misguided. The fact was, had the consummation of their marriage happened any other way, except in such a hot, wild manner, Kelsey probably would have had time to think about it, weighed the pros and cons and lost her nerve. And that would have been a shame because, whether the two of them were really married or not, she wouldn't trade the experience for anything. She rolled over, so she was lying on his chest, looking up at him. Unable to keep herself from touching him even one second longer, she ran her fingers through the tufts of dark hair on his chest and looked up at him earnestly. "That was exactly the way I wanted it to happen, Brady. It was exciting and—" she flushed, but forced herself to continue "—wonderful...."

He smiled at her unabashed praise and reached over to gently brush the hair from her cheek and kiss the back of her hand. "Still—"

"Still, nothing," Kelsey interrupted, scooting closer yet. She draped one of her legs between the warmth of his. "I know I'm inexperienced here, Brady. Not as inexperienced as I was—" she grinned mischievously as one hand drifted playfully lower "—but inexperienced nevertheless." She paused, looked deep into his eyes, before continuing seriously, "But I'm also an adult who's been on my own for a long time now. I know what I wanted, Brady. And what I wanted was you," she said softly, earnestly.

"I wanted you, too. Still do, as a matter of fact."

He moved so he was on top of her once again. The possessive look in his eyes made her catch her breath. She could blame their first bout of love-making on a combination of passion and recklessness. If they made love again, the way he clearly wanted to make love to her, slowly and deliberately, it was bound to mean much more. It was bound to make her fall all the way in love with him.

Kelsey wasn't sure she was ready for that. She wasn't sure she was ready to let him all the way into her heart. Because doing that would make her vulnerable in a way she'd never been before. She swallowed around the sudden lump of emotion in her throat. "Brady—" she whispered tremulously.

"I'll be a lot more gentle this time," he whispered, mistaking the reason for her unease. "I promise."

It was all Kelsey could do not to sigh at the languid nature of his touch. She pouted as his hands moved over her, butterfly soft, accommodating. "I don't want you to be gentle." She didn't want him protecting her. She wanted to be his partner, his equal, in every way. But Brady, it seemed, had ideas of his own.

He grinned, already bending his head and kissing her thoroughly. "Tell me that after, and I'll believe you," he teased. "Until then, we'll do this on my time frame, my way."

Chapter 10

"Brady's way" turned out to be wonderful, sensual and slow. By the time morning came, and they finally fell asleep, wrapped in each other's arms, Kelsey had never felt so well-loved, so treasured and wanted, in her life. And unless she missed her guess, Brady was just as happy with the way she made love to him, too.

So happy that when they woke the next morning, he couldn't seem to stop smiling any more than she could. "I think we should move all your stuff up to the house and put it in the master bedroom, along with mine," Kelsey said as they shared a breakfast of coffee and cinnamon rolls on the front porch and watched the sun rise.

"That's a pretty big step," Brady said, wrapping his arm around her.

Kelsey turned to him with a contented smile. "I know." But it felt right to her. And for now, that was all that was important.

Brady grinned and kissed the top of her head. "Well, just for the record, it suits me just fine."

Together, they brought his belongings— which consisted of a steamer trunk of clothes and books—to the house, and put them away. As they worked, Kelsey couldn't help but compare his meager belongings to the amount of stuff she had accumulated over the years. She'd heard about traveling light, but this was ridiculous, she thought. Surely he had more stuff somewhere.

And if not, why not?

"What are you thinking about?" Brady asked as he hung the last of his shirts in the closet, next to her shirts and jeans.

The last thing Kelsey wanted to do was put a damper on the happiness she'd found. She had a feeling asking Brady questions he had always been loathe to answer would do just that. She'd find out what she needed to know in time, she reassured herself firmly. All she had to do was be patient. Even if patience wasn't a virtue that came easily to her. "I was thinking about how much work we have to do today," Kelsey said, glancing out the window at the clouds gathering on the horizon. "The saddles and horses and cattle are going to be delivered this morning and it looks like a blue norther is rolling in."

Brady switched on the weather radio beside Kelsey's bed. It ran on batteries and only got one channel—the national weather service for their area. Forecasts were broadcast continuously.

"The cold front coming down from the north is bringing a twenty-degree drop in temperatures and a ninety percent chance of rain," the forecaster said. "The precipitation should continue throughout the night, ending by midmorning tomorrow...."

"Darn it," Kelsey said, shaking her head in frustration as she met Brady's eyes. "That means I'm going to have to cancel this afternoon's after-school riding lessons."

"What you need is a covered arena, so your lessons can go on no matter what," Brady said. He took her by the hand and led her outside, and showed her where he thought it should go. "It probably wouldn't take long to build, either."

"If we had the money," Kelsey concurred, looking at the spot Brady had picked out behind the stables. She turned to him with a sigh. "We've just about spent everything Wade lent us." They had enough for feed and vet bills, to get them through until the real money started coming in, but that was about it.

"You leave that to me." Brady leaned over and kissed her tenderly on the lips. As the sky darkened ominously all the more, he led her back inside. "Right now we have more important things to think about," he said.

As Brady set about pouring them more coffee, Kelsey pushed away the memories the dark clouds brought. That was how the sky had looked the day her parents had been killed in the tornado. Even though no tornado warnings had been issued, she felt a sense of foreboding, anyway.

Pushing her superstitious fear away—nothing bad was going to happen—not when she had just found the kind of all-encompassing love she had always wanted, just like her sisters had. She rubbed her arms briskly, to ward off the chill that had overtaken her. She accepted the mug from Brady and forced herself to smile at him. "And what important things would those be—besides waiting for the delivery trucks that are bringing our new horses and cattle?"

He held out her chair for her, then snapped up a pad and pen off the kitchen counter, before he sat down with her at the kitchen table. "We need to figure out what our brand is going to be."

Kelsey had been putting off a decision on that for several months now. It hadn't seemed important since they didn't have much stock. Now that was about to change, she figured they were going to have to come to some decision. And soon. She hesitated, wondering if they were going to be able to agree about this. "We can't use the sideways L my parents used to have—we let the registration lapse when we sold the ranch years ago and it's since been taken up by someone else."

"Maybe that's for the best, anyway," Brady said as he put up his arm, blocking her view of whatever it was he was drawing on the page in front of him. "Given the fact that the two of us are starting fresh and going into business together."

Kelsey studied him. Brady was one of the most deliberate men she knew. If he had brought this up, it was because he had made a decision. "You have something in mind, don't you?"

"Mmm-hmm." He continued drawing, then turned the page over so she could see. "What do you think?"

Kelsey studied the two interlocking hearts, with the arrow that went through them both. "Even sort of makes sense," Brady continued, then explained what he was proposing with a heart-stoppingly sexy smile. "Locked hearts. Lockhart."

Kelsey flushed at the unexpectedly romantic nature of his suggestion. "I like it. As long as it's not taken."

"It isn't." Brady sat back in his chair, looking confident as all get-out. "I checked. So what do you say?" He looked deep into her eyes. "You want to register that as our brand?"

Yes, Kelsey thought. *You don't know how much. Mostly because of how much it seems to indicate you care about me and think of us as a couple now.*

But almost as soon as she thought it, the practical side of her disagreed with the emotions of her heart. Adapting a brand like that set the bar pretty high for them. Since her parents had died, Kelsey had made a habit of setting the bar low, so she wouldn't be crushed if her hopes and dreams didn't match the reality of what actually occurred. She bit her lip, searching for an excuse that would allow him to back out gracefully, before they made even bigger fools of themselves than most people—including her family and the McCabe clan—thought she already had. "I don't know, Brady." Kelsey traced her finger around the rim of her coffee mug. "The other ranchers in the area might have a heyday with this."

Brady shrugged his broad shoulders affably,

as confident he was going to get what he wanted in the end, as ever. "Let 'em tease me for being romantic. I don't care who knows you stole my heart, Kelse, 'cause you have." He leaned across the table, took her hands in his and kissed her, sweetly and tenderly. The next thing she knew she was sitting on his lap. His arms were all the way around her. And he was still kissing her with a passion and a gentleness she had never guessed might exist when they heard the sound of a vehicle rumbling up the drive. "That's probably one of our deliveries," Kelsey said, reluctantly starting to break it off.

"Let 'em wait," Brady murmured around another kiss. "Can't they see I'm busy here?"

Kelsey giggled and let him draw her even further into the embrace. Before she knew it, Kelsey had forgotten all about their visitor, and she was kissing him back, at first sweetly and tenderly, then with building passion. One kiss turned into two, two turned into three. Brady wrapped his arms around her more tightly, bringing her closer yet. She arched against him, her breasts crushed against the powerful muscles of his chest.

"Well, seems like I owe you five bucks after all," a familiar feminine voice said.

Kelsey and Brady turned to see Dani and Beau standing by the porch. Dani shook her head, tacitly accepting blame where it was due. "Beau's been saying for months now that the two of you were seriously, romantically attracted to each other," she said. "I was thinking it was just a friendship, and a pretty casual one at that. Seems he was right," Dani continued as she and Beau came all the way up the porch, an overflowing gift basket in hand. "And it also seems I owe you an apology, Kelsey." Hand to her pregnant tummy, she backed into the chair Beau held out for her and set the gift basket on the kitchen table. "I am so sorry I got upset about the computer."

"It's okay." Kelsey waved off her older sister's concern as she slid off Brady's lap. "I shouldn't have broken it."

"You didn't break it," Brady interrupted, pulling her right back into his lap and anchoring his arms around her waist. "It broke on you, remember?"

Kelsey wished she could be as sure as her husband was about that.

"He's right," Dani said firmly, exchanging matter-of-fact looks of apology with everyone in the room. "That computer has been giving me trouble off and on for months now. I just didn't take the time to get it looked at. And I'm really sorry I started crying and everything." She teared up again just talking about it, and fished for a tissue in the pocket of her chic maternity pantsuit. "I've just been really emotional the past few months."

"I can attest to that," Beau said, gently patting Dani's shoulder. "She's even started crying at the commercials on TV."

"Well, some of them are pretty sentimental," Kelsey pointed out in Dani's defense.

"The ones about floor wax?" Beau teased.

"Beau's right. I have been weeping a lot at strange moments," Dani said. "The doctor says it's hormones. Anyway…" Dani handed over a basket of goodies for Kelsey and Brady. It was filled with an assortment of gourmet cheeses, wine and fruit, as well as a freshly baked loaf of sourdough bread. "I wanted to make sure we were okay, 'cause I don't want to fight with you, Kelsey."

"I don't want to fight with you, either," Kelsey said.

The two stood, and Kelsey and Dani hugged as best they could around Dani's pregnant tummy. Dani looked at Kelsey as they drew apart. "You really are happy, aren't you?" she said softly, looking as pleased as Kelsey was about that.

"Yes." Kelsey smiled. "I am."

And no one was more surprised about that than she was.

Kelsey and Brady spent the rest of the day making sure the cattle got unloaded to the appropriate pastures, the new horses put in the stable, and the saddles and tack stored for cleaning and repair as soon as they could get to it. They didn't eat dinner until after nine, and by 10:00 p.m., they were exhausted and ready for bed when the doorbell rang.

To their amazement, Rafe Marshall was standing on their doorstep. He was dressed in a suit and tie, and looked more miserable than Kelsey could ever recall seeing him. Rafe looked at Brady. "About last night—"

"Kelsey explained."

"Good." Rafe gave Brady a man-to-man look. "I wouldn't want to be responsible for any trouble between the two of you."

"You haven't been," Kelsey said.

"In fact, if anything, you helped us get a few things straight," Brady said, looking at Kelsey. He turned back to Rafe and shook his hand, then ushered him in out of the rain and chill November wind. "So it all worked out in the end."

"I'm glad," Rafe said, looking happy for them but no less miserable himself.

Kelsey took Rafe's overcoat and hung it on the rack next to the door to dry. She had only to look at his face to know he had bad news. "What's wrong?" she asked, concerned.

Rafe sat down in front of the fire Brady had built. "When I took Patricia to the Gilded Lily tonight, we had the same maître d' you and I had last night."

Kelsey tensed as she and Brady took a seat on the sofa. "The snooty, sarcastic one?"

"Yep. He recognized me instantly, and he pulled me aside before he seated us, and said he was glad to see me but that he hoped the woman I was with tonight was not married to someone else because he didn't want any more ugly scenes. Patricia overheard, and she marched out of the restaurant before we could even be seated."

Kelsey flattened a hand across her heart. "Oh, no."

"'Oh, no' is right," Rafe agreed miserably, looking at both Brady and Kelsey. "I tried explaining to her that it wasn't what she thought, but all she wanted to know was one thing, had I been with someone else last night who was indeed married to someone else. And when I confirmed that was so, she cut me off and demanded I take her home."

"Did you at least explain everything to her?"

Rafe shook his head, sighed heavily. "There was no point. She just wasn't going to listen. Besides, I didn't want to make things worse for you, and at this point, no one in Laramie knows what you and I did except Brady and he's not telling anyone. Are you?"

"I haven't," Brady confirmed. "But I do think

you ought to just spill all to Patricia and let the chips fall where they may."

"I agree," Kelsey said. "Honesty is always the best policy."

"I'm sure she'll understand," Brady continued.

Rafe and Kelsey exchanged troubled looks.

"Okay, I'm missing something here," Brady concluded quickly. "What is it?"

"Patricia was involved with a married man before she came to Laramie," Kelsey explained. "The whole experience has left her kind of gun-shy when it comes to men."

"The bottom line is I blew it with her, just like I figured I would," Rafe continued. "I just wanted you two to know what happened, and that I protected Kelsey and her reputation. No one knows she was the woman there with me, and no one has to know."

"That's where you're wrong," Kelsey said. "Someone has to talk to Patricia and set her straight. And it's going to be me. I'll go and see her first thing tomorrow morning."

Rafe Marshall left shortly after. Brady would have thought that would have been that, as far as Kelsey was concerned, since nothing more could be done that evening, but it wasn't. Her mood was as down as Rafe's had been.

Figuring there was something there that needed to be talked about, Brady added another log to the fire in the fireplace to ward off the chill of the evening and brought out the bottle of wine that had been in the basket Beau and Dani had delivered earlier in the day. "Okay, tell me what's on your mind," he coaxed as he poured them both a glass of chardonnay.

Kelsey was a complicated woman. Brady wanted to understand her as badly as he felt she secretly wanted to be understood. But that wasn't going to happen unless she let him. And right now, for everything she said to him, she still kept twice as much to herself. Of course, he could hardly criticize her, given what he had yet to tell her about his identity and his past, Brady thought.

"It's nothing," Kelsey insisted. She took a sip of her wine, then put it back on the coffee table in front of her.

"It is something if it has you looking that unhappy," Brady disagreed as he sat down beside her.

Kelsey gave him a look that let him know she didn't appreciate his goading. Tough, Brady thought. He wasn't giving up until he found out what was bothering her. "If you want to play twenty questions, we can do it that way."

Kelsey blew out an exasperated breath and leapt

up from the sofa. Both hands shoved in the back pockets of her jeans, she began to pace.

Abruptly, she whirled to face him and said in a low, dead-serious tone, "If you're smart, you'll get out while the going is still good."

Brady blinked, sure he hadn't heard right. "What?"

Kelsey lifted both hands in a helpless gesture, then let them fall again to her sides. Moisture gleamed in her pretty green eyes. "I'm jinxed." She swallowed hard and, her eyes locked with his, continued explaining sadly, "You've heard of Wade McCabe, and how everything he touches magically turns to gold?" she asked softly. "Well, everything I touch turns to rust."

Brady would have laughed at the ridiculous notion, had she not been so pale. "You're serious," he whispered.

Kelsey nodded. She wiped her damp eyes with the back of her hand and said in a low, trembling voice, "And with good reason. This situation with Rafe is only the last in a long line of catastrophes, the only common denominator in all of them being me." The tears she had been suppressing fell in a torrent, spilling over her cheeks and chin. "My parents died because I wasn't where I was supposed to be and they were out looking for me."

"That was a random act of fate, Kelsey."

"I might believe that, too, if it were only that incident." Kelsey shoved her hands through her hair. "But there have been dozens of them since."

"Such as...?"

"I knew about Jenna's botched elopement to Jake when they were teenagers. I could have stopped it, Brady. If I had, his parents might never have found out about it and taken action to separate them, and they might never have been apart."

Brady hadn't been around when that happened, but he had heard the story at the time Jenna and Jake had gotten married this past summer. "That was years ago, Kelse. You were just a kid yourself."

"So? There's no age limit on jinxes, Brady. I'm bad luck, pure and simple." She studied him in obvious frustration. "You don't believe me, do you?"

Brady shook his head. "No." He stood and tried to take her in his arms, but she pushed him away.

"Maybe you would if you had been around when Meg delivered Jeremy."

Brady leaned against the mantel. He studied the color in her face and the anguish in her eyes. Was this guilt the root of her recklessness? Was it fear behind her legendary fickleness, instead of just an inability to make up her mind or commit to any one person or thing? "What happened there?" he asked calmly, wanting—needing—to know how all these pieces fit together for her.

Kelsey sat down again on the sofa. She gulped her wine. "Meg went into premature labor when we were returning home from a shopping trip together."

Brady watched the way her fingers tightened on the stem of her glass. "I suppose you did something to Dani, too?"

Kelsey nodded, her knuckles turning as white as her face. "I'm the one who talked Dani into going off to Mexico with Beau Chamberlain to help settle their feud." She took another gulp of wine. "They came back married."

Brady shrugged and countered calmly, "They look happy enough now."

"They weren't at first!" She set her glass back down on the coffee table. Distress tightened the pretty features of her face. "In fact, due to some weird happenings down there, neither of them could even remember saying 'I do.'"

Brady had heard about that, too—everyone in Laramie had. "The fact they both had amnesia about their wedding was not your fault," Brady said sternly. Guessing what she was about to say next, he said, "And neither was the fact her laptop broke while you were using it."

"Yeah, well—" Kelsey shivered, looking as if

she would never be warm again "—tell that to her the next time something happens and it can't be fixed so easily. Tell that to Rafe, who probably had a clear shot to Patricia Weatherby's heart until I got involved." New tears spilled down Kelsey's cheeks.

Brady went back to the sofa and sat down beside her. He shifted her resisting body onto his lap and cuddled her against him. He pressed a kiss into her hair. "You're going to fix that tomorrow, we both are, when we talk to Patricia and tell her straight out what happened and why." Brady paused. He tucked his fingers beneath her chin and tilted her head up to his. "As for everything else, in every life a little rain must fall. You can view the catastrophes that come up as problems and give up. Or you can view them as challenges and take 'em on, one right after another." He flashed her a crooked grin designed to lift her spirits. "You know what I prefer."

She let out a wistful breath and slowly began to smile. "You like the challenges."

"Yep." Brady threaded his hands through her hair, glad she had come to her senses once again. "And most of all, I like you. You're my favorite challenge, Kelse," he told her solemnly, loving the way she nestled against him. "The one I want to win, and dedicate myself to, more than anything else."

Warm amusement sparkled in her eyes as she splayed her hands across his chest, rubbing, stroking. Reckless as ever, she said, "You think you've won me."

Brady noticed she didn't quibble with his desire to dedicate himself to making her happy. Deciding it was time they curtailed the talk and switched to action that would better prove the way he felt about her, he shifted her so she was lying against the back of the sofa. He stretched out beside her, cupped her cheek and gently ran his thumb along her lips.

"Famous last words," he teased. "Especially since there's not a challenge that's gotten the best of me yet. You included, sweetheart."

Kelsey grinned all the more. "Well, maybe I'll be the first," she murmured softly, already unbuttoning his shirt.

"I don't think so." He took her face in his hands and kissed her with the same deep and abiding hunger she felt. Her lips softened under his, inviting him into her sweet, urgent heat. But when he wanted her undressed, it was Kelsey who took the lead, helping him with his clothes. Touching and kissing him with a wild sensuality that surprised him, even as it pushed him toward the edge. Not about to go without her, he shifted so she was beneath him once again. Together, they dispensed with her clothes. The orange-blossom scent of her hair and skin drove him wild, and their kisses, fed by a passion that had taken on a life of its own, took on an even wilder flavor.

"Now," she said, urging him closer.

"Not," Brady decided, "until I've had my fill."

She shut her eyes as he took her hands and anchored them on either side of her head. "I can't wait that long," she whispered.

"Yes, you can," he whispered back, loving how much she wanted him. "And I'll prove it to you."

Ignoring her hoarse exclamation of need, he held her wrists in one hand and used his other to touch, stroke, love. She trembled and he kissed her again, taking her mouth with his, until the mating of their tongues was an intimate act without an ounce of restraint. Her skin grew hot and flushed, and her thighs splayed wide to accommodate his legs. His sex pressed against her, and a fierce wave of tenderness swept through him. He hadn't expected her to be so vulnerable—ever. She was. He hadn't expected her to be so open to loving him. But she made him feel like he was hers and hers alone.

Knowing, even if she didn't, that she was the one who was conquering him, he flicked her nip-

ples with his tongue and touched her with his lips
and explored her with his hands, until she was
silky wet and trembling. Ready. Wanting. Needing. Parting her knees with his, he braced a hand
on either side of her and situated himself between
her thighs. Her hands caught his hips, brought
him against her, closed around him and guided
him inside. The last of his restraint fell away as
she drove him to the brink. He moved inside her,
commanding everything she had to give, while
at the same time availing every part of him to
her. They were married. They were part of each
other. And for the first time, the only time in his
life, Brady learned what it was like to be with a
woman, heart and soul. He hadn't known he could
want like that. He hadn't known he could need.
But he did. And so, he thought, as their climax
inevitably came, did she.

They floated there, breathing hard and clinging
to each other. Enjoying the aftershocks consuming
their bodies, Brady touched his lips to her face,
her hair. She was so sweet. So wild. And she was
all his. Which left them only one thing to resolve.
He shifted so he could see her face, and she could
see his. "Still feel like a jinx?" he asked her softly.

"No." Kelsey let out a trembling sigh as she
pressed a kiss into his palm, gratitude and affec-

tion shimmering in her eyes. "Not anymore," she told him confidently.

"Good," Brady said, his satisfaction complete. He tightened his arms around her possessively. "'Cause you're the best thing that ever happened to me, Kelse." No question.

Chapter 11

The phone rang the next morning as they were walking out the door. "Let the answering machine take it," Brady said.

"Okay, but I just want to listen to the message in case it's anything important," Kelsey said as the prerecorded message clicked on, followed by the beep and a man's voice. "It's Friday morning. This is Hargett. Brady, I want to talk to you about our…situation."

Frowning, Brady pushed by Kelsey and headed for the machine.

"Look, I know I said I'd give you the full two weeks you've got left," Hargett continued gruffly, "but I just can't. Not after the way we left things the other morning. I want to talk to you about the money and everything else you promised me, ASAP—"

Brady clicked the stop button on the machine, then turned the answering machine off entirely so no further messages would be recorded in their absence.

"Why did you do that?" Kelsey demanded as the phone began to ring again a few minutes later.

Brady pushed her out the door and locked it behind them. "Because I know what he's going to say."

"Well, I don't!" Kelsey argued.

Brady fixed her with a warning glance. "The message isn't for you, Kelsey."

"In other words," Kelsey guessed, unable to help but feel hurt at the way he was shutting her out of whatever was going on with Hargett, as the phone continued to ring, as insistently as ever, "I should mind my own business." And that hurt, because she'd thought Brady understood, accepted and appreciated her like no one else. Had she been wrong about that? And if so, what else was she wrong about? Kelsey wondered.

Brady sighed. Obviously realizing how upset she was, he closed the distance between them and cupped her shoulders gently. "Look, Hargett is a complex guy. What problems the two of us have are between him and me. I know you want to help me deal with him, but—" the hesitation was back in his voice "—the bottom line is, you can't."

Kelsey began to feel very uneasy. Brady was acting as if whatever Hargett said or did could somehow hurt the two of them and/or disrupt the happiness they'd found as man and wife. She swallowed hard. She wasn't worried about herself. She had the feeling she could handle Hargett. But she didn't want anything to happen to Brady. She cared about him too much. "Is he threatening you?" she asked warily.

Brady's mouth tightened into a grim line. His eyes took on a remote look. "Not the way you think," he said bluntly.

Kelsey thought about all the options and finally concluded, "He wants something from you, doesn't he? That's why he keeps calling and coming around."

Brady turned his brooding glance to her and admitted, with a great deal of reluctance, "He wants me to go back to work for him."

"Doing what?"

"Just…business," Brady said vaguely, looking all the more evasive and uncomfortable. "It's not anything I want to do. And it's not important to the two of us, 'cause it's not going to happen."

Kelsey studied him wordlessly. There was something he still wasn't telling her. And didn't want her to know, Kelsey decided. "Maybe it's not important to you," she said, hurt at the way Brady kept refusing to confide in her.

Brady's lips tightened in exasperation. "There is nothing that Hargett has to say to me that won't keep until I'm of a mind to deal with him," he said grimly. "And that'll come soon enough."

Seeing the worry come back into his dark blue eyes, Kelsey felt her uneasiness grow by leaps and bounds. "Look, I know you've gotten in over your head. And I just want you to know I don't blame you," Kelsey continued hastily, putting up a silencing hand before he could interrupt her. "It could have happened to anyone who needed money and had nowhere else to borrow it. And heaven knows we've had to sink a lot more than we thought into the house, bringing it back to a livable state. But it's not too late, Brady. There's still a way out. There's always a way out."

Brady studied her with obvious admiration and gratitude. "You'd forgive me," he questioned thoughtfully, "even knowing I did something to compromise my future?"

"Yes," Kelsey said firmly. "I would."

"You're some kind of woman, Kelsey," Brady said with obvious admiration.

"Thank you." Kelsey beamed at his praise.

"But we still don't need to discuss this here and now," Brady decided firmly. "What we do need to do is hurry and get to town if we want to catch Patricia Weatherby before she leaves for work at the chamber of commerce. Otherwise, she's going to think we stood her up."

"All right," Kelsey conceded reluctantly, unable to shake the feeling that trouble was just over the horizon. "But just so you know, Brady, we're not finished talking about this."

Brady knew he should have told Kelsey who Hargett was and what he really wanted from him, aside from going back to work for Hargett and the company, that was. But he hadn't because he knew she'd probably be furious when she found out everything he had been keeping from her and everyone else in Laramie. He was going to have to tell her, of course. And soon, given both the upcoming deadline he and Hargett had agreed upon when Brady had broken away, and the way Hargett was now breathing down his neck.

But he didn't want to tell her.

He didn't want anything to spoil the miracle the two of them had found. And he sensed, from the way Kelsey wasn't really pushing him to confess all here and now, that Kelsey didn't want anything to spoil their newfound love affair and "marriage of convenience," either.

Not when they had a chance to make it all as real and solid and wonderful as the ranch they were now calling home.

They caught up with Patricia at nine-thirty. Her daughter, Molly, was already in school. Patricia wasn't due to work over at the chamber of commerce until ten. "You're here to talk to me about Rafe, aren't you?" she said as she ushered Brady and Kelsey inside. She looked tired and stressed. "Well, you can forget it," she stated emphatically. "I'm not going to go out with anyone who sees a married woman on the side."

Glad she had wasted no time in getting to Patricia, Kelsey hastened to set the record straight. "I was the married woman Rafe was with that night, and it was not a real date, it was a practice date for his evening with you."

Patricia blinked in confusion. "I don't understand. Why would Rafe need a practice date?"

Kelsey rolled her eyes. "Because he's such a klutz and he hasn't dated anyone in a very long time and he has a wild crush on you and he really wanted everything to go just right. He thought if he had a trial run with me, I could critique him and then everything with you would go super smoothly. He really wanted to impress you. And he needed to get his confidence up to do that. That's all it was, Patricia."

"But the waiter said something about a husband coming in, being very upset—"

"That was me," Brady said, owning up to his actions matter-of-factly. "Kelsey neglected to tell me what was going on, and I got the wrong idea. So, yeah, I was pretty jealous until Kelsey explained the situation. The point is, Rafe and Kelsey are just friends, Patricia. I wouldn't be here, asking you to give Rafe Marshall a second chance, if there was anything else going on."

Patricia sat down, her expression bleak. "Oh, dear. What a mess. I imagine, if I'd only given him half a chance, Rafe would have told me all this last night."

"What happened in the past, including last night, isn't important," Brady said. "The future is."

"Did you mean what you said about the future?" Kelsey asked Brady as they turned into the path that led up to the ranch house. "About it being more important than anything that happened in the past, even yesterday?"

Brady nodded as he parked in front of the ranch house and cut the motor on his pickup. He wondered what Kelsey was trying to get up the nerve to ask him.

"Because there's something I need to tell you," she said. She bit into her lower lip uncertainly. "Something important."

Before she could elaborate further, Brady heard another car. He turned and saw a familiar late-model Cadillac coming up the drive. He swore beneath his breath. Kelsey looked just as distressed at the ill-timed interruption.

"Let me take care of this," Brady said firmly. Darn it all. He should have known that Hargett wouldn't stop with a phone message, that he would show up here in person.

Brady climbed out of the pickup truck just as Hargett climbed out of the Cadillac. The two met halfway. Brady blew out an exasperated breath as he regarded their uninvited guest. "You want to see me, fine, but not here and not now."

"Then when?" Hargett demanded unhappily as Kelsey dashed out of the pickup and threw herself between them.

"To get to him, you're going to have to go through me," she vowed.

Hargett's brows drew together. As before, he was dressed in an elegant and expensive business suit, seemingly at odds with his rough-hewn appearance. "Is that so?" Hargett drawled, regarding Brady's wife with obvious amusement.

"Yes." Kelsey kept her arms out on either side

of her and backed up until she was totally blocking Hargett's access to Brady. "Listen here, Hargett, I don't know what it is that you've got hanging over Brady's head, but I think you should just forget about getting him to come back to work for you, and go home."

Brady clamped his hands on her shoulders and attempted to move her, so she was no longer shielding him with her body. "Kelsey, you don't have to defend me here," he said, frustrated at the way Kelsey was digging in her heels and refusing to budge.

"Actually," Hargett interrupted, raising his brow and folding his arms in front of him, "I want to hear what this wife of yours has to say, Brady. I admire a gal with gumption. Plus, unless I am mistaken, and I don't think I am, this little filly really loves you."

"I'm not a filly, but you're right, I do love him," Kelsey retorted hotly.

And I love you, Brady thought. But he wasn't telling Kelsey that. Not here and not now. Not in front of Hargett. That could wait until they were alone and had a properly romantic setting, so he could kiss and hold Kelsey the way he wanted to kiss and hold her when he told her he loved her for the very first time.

"And I want to protect him from the likes of you," Kelsey argued hotly.

Hargett laughed.

Brady glared at him. Of all the times he didn't need the kind of interference Hargett was capable of, it was now. "I will talk to you later," he promised again, looking at Hargett. "Right now, you need to leave," he stated emphatically.

But instead of leaving, Hargett said, frowning, "You didn't tell her who I was, did you?"

At that, it was all Brady could do not to cringe. He swore beneath his breath. "No. I didn't. Not yet."

"Which means she doesn't know who you really are, either," Hargett concluded heavily, with a telling, sympathetic look at Kelsey. "Does she?"

Hargett and Brady might as well have been talking in secret code, for all Kelsey was getting of their conversation. "Of course I know who he is!" Kelsey retorted, reassuring herself there was absolutely no need for her to panic, despite the secretive glances Brady and Hargett were exchanging. "He's Brady Anderson. My husband." She pressed a hand to her heart and continued in a low, fiercely emotional tone of voice. "And I love him with all my heart and soul."

"I think you've done enough damage here," Brady told Hargett tightly.

"I'm not the one who kept something that important from my wife," Hargett countered, looking Brady up and down. "But you're right, Brady. This is a discussion you and Kelsey should have alone. When you've finished, call me at the inn. Or come by and see me in person. Like I said on the phone, we have some very important business to discuss." He handed Brady a small card, with a phone number scribbled on the back. He tipped his hat at Kelsey, went back to his Cadillac, climbed in and drove away. Kelsey stared at Brady, waiting for the explanation to come.

Brady sighed, swept off his hat and slammed it against his thigh. His jaw was clenched. He looked and acted as frustrated and upset as Kelsey suddenly felt. "That was my dad." He pushed the words through his teeth.

As the meaning of Brady's words sank in, Kelsey felt like she'd just had all the air knocked out of her lungs. "Your dad," she repeated, stunned.

"Yes." Brady clenched his jaw all the more. He turned and looked Kelsey square in the eye. "His full name is Hargett Anderson and he owns the Anderson Oil Company."

Kelsey's knees grew weak. "Not the same company that owns all those gas stations."

"One and the same."

She leaned against the back of Brady's pickup truck. "And you're an heir to all that?"

"Not just an heir." Brady's midnight-blue eyes glimmered with barely checked resentment. "The *only* heir."

Kelsey worked to contain her hurt, even as she struggled to understand why Brady had done what he had. "Why didn't you tell me?" she whispered.

Brady slammed his hat back on his head and tugged the brim low across his forehead. "Because for the last two years I have been trying to live a normal life, the kind of life I never had the chance to live as a kid."

"Your father disapproved of that?"

"Yes. He grew up dirt poor. He had no connections. He had to do everything on his own and he sees no reason why I should have to do the same when he could hand it all to me on a silver platter."

"But you don't want to help him run his company."

Brady frowned. "I've got the talent to do it, no question."

Kelsey recalled what a fierce bargainer he was. How he cared about every aspect of the business, and always watched the bottom line.

"I just wasn't happy as an oil company exec," Brady continued, as if willing her to understand. "Dad thought it was a phase, that I would get over my need to be my own man and blaze my own path. But I knew that wasn't the case. I not only had what it took to be a cowboy, but to own my own ranch as well. Anyway, I made this deal with my dad. He had to stop pressuring me and totally stay out of my life during the two years I was proving my mettle. If I couldn't do it, learn the business and save enough money to purchase a ranch of my own and make it a success, then at the end of that time I would go back to Houston and spend the rest of my life working for him and the company again."

"So that's why you were so desperate to go into partnership with me and make this ranch work," Kelsey supposed slowly, "even if it meant borrowing money from Wade McCabe to stock it."

Brady shot her an irritated look. "I could have bought a ranch of my own."

"Not one this big," Kelsey countered, mocking his mildly irritated tone. She glared at him, not sure whether she was more hurt or angry, just knowing she was both. "Not without my seed money, too." How could he have kept something this important from her, even after Hargett started coming around and while he knew she was worried about Hargett's interference, the way he seemed to be pressuring Brady?

Brady stubbornly held his ground. "I thought we'd be good together. I wanted this ranch to be a success for both of us, Kelsey."

"When were you going to tell me?" Kelsey demanded.

"Soon," Brady said vaguely.

"Today?" Kelsey pressed, as impatient to get to the truth as he was reluctant to give it.

Brady shrugged, as if that hardly mattered. "I probably would have waited a few more days," he conceded after a minute.

"Or in other words, as long as possible," Kelsey guessed.

"Or until I'd gotten my trust fund."

Kelsey's heart sank. Just when she thought it couldn't get any worse, she found out there was yet another element to Brady's duplicity.

"I'm due to come into my trust fund in a little over a week now—that's the deadline Hargett keeps referring to," Brady continued. "My getting the funds was contingent upon my being a success as a rancher. That's why I wasn't worried about paying Wade McCabe back, or building an indoor arena or anything else, because I knew I'd have the money to do anything we wanted to do here if I just made it a few more weeks."

"You must've really wanted this," Kelsey said as a chill descended over her heart.

Brady nodded affirmatively. "There's a lot we can do with those funds to continue to fix up this place, Kelsey. Heck, with that kind of money, we could go state-of-the-art on everything and make the Lockhart-Anderson Ranch a real showplace."

Kelsey had once thought Brady's ambition and ability to dream big were laudable. That was before she had been used to further both. "Well, I have to hand it to you, Brady," Kelsey said bitterly. "You made a complete and utter fool out of me. Here I thought you'd done all this because you wanted me as your partner so we could build something real and lasting. When all I ever was was the means to an end."

Brady released a short, impatient breath and gave her a look that said she was making this unnecessarily hard on them both. "You can't seriously believe that," he said.

The problem was, she did. Not once, Kelsey recalled, had Brady ever said he loved her. Or even could be falling in love with her. Not once had he hinted that he wanted their marriage to be anything more than a furthering of the business arrangement and the friendship they already had.

Once, she'd thought those things would be enough to make her happy. But that had been before she'd fallen in love with Brady. Now she needed him to love her, too. If he didn't… Well, Kelsey didn't see any reason to continue on with an arrangement that was only going to devastate her in the end. She looked at him steadily, wanting him to come to grips with the harsh reality of the situation, too. "You needed me to make your dreams of owning your own ranch come true."

Brady's face hardened. "I needed you for a lot more than that, Kelsey."

"Yeah," Kelsey agreed sarcastically, remembering how wonderful it had been when they'd been together in bed. "You needed me for passion. Fun. Companionship." But not as a real wife. Tears stung her eyes. "No wonder your father was so disapproving and so upset to find you here with me. He knew all along what you were up to even when I had no clue." It was funny, in a sad sort of way. For so long she'd been afraid to give her heart to anyone, for fear she'd get hurt. When she finally had put that fear aside and given her heart to Brady Anderson, she'd ended up devastated, anyway. How ironic was that?

"Don't use my father as an excuse. Yes, he's a pain. But Hargett's not the problem here, Kelsey. You are. You don't even have to tell me. I can see it by the look on your face. You've got one foot out the door already, don't you?"

Kelsey didn't want to hear Brady spout off what everyone else already thought—that she was so naturally fickle she couldn't be trusted to love anyone. Because that wasn't what had happened here. Brady had betrayed her, not the other way around. "You can't seriously expect me to stay in this marriage, knowing what I know now!"

Brady glared at her. "You just told my father that you loved me," he reminded her grimly. "Or was that all a lie?"

Kelsey hurt, just thinking how quickly she had jumped to his defense. She stared at Brady in confusion. "I didn't even know who you really were," she reminded him quietly, abruptly feeling as confused and adrift as she had when she and Brady had first met the previous summer, when they had both been ranch hands on Travis McCabe's ranch. "So how could I love you?" she asked him sadly. "How could I love anything we've done together or been to each other when none of it, absolutely none of it, has been real?"

Brady looked away a long moment, before returning his gaze to her. "Great excuse, Kelse. But it doesn't wash with me. You're just looking for a way out because you're scared to make a commitment."

Kelsey didn't feel that way at all. But, she figured uneasily, maybe he did. And that hurt her more than she could possibly say. "You'd like to blame this all on me," she stated angrily, "but I'm not going to make it that simple for you. You know what I think?" Kelsey demanded, stomping closer, not stopping until they stood toe-to-toe and nose-to-nose. "I think you're the one who wants out of our marriage of convenience, Brady. Not telling me who you were was just a way of providing yourself with the insurance to do just that, once you had met your father's terms and gotten your inheritance, of course."

Brady regarded her stoically. "I'm not that cold-blooded, Kelsey."

"Maybe not consciously," Kelsey allowed, feeling as if her heart were breaking. "But the bottom line is still the bottom line, in ranching or relationships or anything else." Able to see he still disagreed, she pushed on deliberately, "You told me yourself how much you like a challenge. And there's no greater challenge around here than winning my heart. It was probably a real test of your mettle, wasn't it?" she asked, unable to keep the bitterness from her voice. "After all, you've gone where no man has ever gone before."

"You asked me to marry you, remember? You invited me to your bed! Furthermore," Brady thundered on brusquely, giving her no chance to interrupt, "I've been a good husband to you."

Kelsey had once thought so, too. But that had been before Brady's father had showed Kelsey just how superficial and shallow her relationship with Brady really was. "Good husbands don't keep secrets from their wives," Kelsey shot back tightly. Good husbands had confidence in their wives.

And damn it all, Brady had known how much his pretending to be something other than what he was, how much his keeping something that important from her, even after they'd started to get close, would hurt. But he had gone on and done it anyway.

Kelsey clamped her arms in front of her and continued to regard him angrily. "Face it, Brady, if you had really cared about me, if you had really wanted this marriage of ours to work, you would never have shut me out this way."

But he had, and that spoke volumes about what was in his heart. The bottom line was he didn't trust her enough to confide in her. And without trust, there could be no love. And love and trust were the two things she wanted most of all.

Brady hooked his thumbs through the belt loops on his jeans and stared down at her with resentment. His mouth tightened into a thin line. "You're saying it's over?"

Kelsey looked at him with unbearable sadness. "Don't you see?" she said quietly. "It has to be."

Chapter 12

"You should have told her who you were before you married her, son," Hargett told Brady later the same day, when Brady went to see Hargett at the country inn where he was staying.

"I think I figured that out already, Dad," Brady said with no small trace of irony in his low voice. Not leveling with Kelsey had been the biggest mistake of his life. He took off his hat and sat down opposite his dad, in one of the wing chairs before the fireplace. "Not that it matters, anyway."

Hargett's eyes narrowed in concern. He gathered the business papers he had been studying when Brady got there, then put them aside. "What do you mean?" he demanded.

Brady's jaw tightened as he thought about what his wife had said to him. Feeling more restless and discontent than ever, he shoved a hand through his hair. "Kelsey's decided to move on to greener pastures."

"And you're just going to let her go?" Hargett asked, disbelief etched in the craggy lines of his face.

Brady didn't see what choice he had. He was hardly going to hog-tie his wife to keep her by his side. Right now, that seemed like the only way he could keep Kelsey. Ten to one, she was booting his belongings out of the house and onto the porch right now.

"So you're just another in a string of guys that have passed through her life," Hargett guessed.

Brady nodded, silently telling himself he would get over this. "Right."

"Bull." Hargett got up and went to the minibar in the corner of the room. He got out two bottles of Lone Star beer, handed one to Brady and twisted off the cap on his own. "I saw the way that wife of yours looked at you, the way she threw herself in front of you to protect you, when she thought I was there to do you harm. That gal loves you, son."

Brady twisted off the cap on his beer and sat

with it cradled in his hand. "Whether she does or not is immaterial," he countered, the icy chill of the glass seeping through to his palm. "She doesn't want to stay with me."

Hargett took a long, thirsty drink. Regret colored his eyes an even darker hue. "Don't make the same mistake I made with your mother."

Brady paused with the bottle halfway to his mouth and put it back down without taking a drink. "What are you talking about?"

Hargett wiped his mouth with the back of his hand. "Your mother was convinced I didn't love her, not the way I should. Instead of making sure she knew how much she meant to me, I told her if she wanted to go she should go. And darn it all if she didn't up and do just that. I should have gone after her. But I didn't," Hargett emphasized in a brusque tone with an even blunter look, "because I was too stubborn and proud. I figured in time she'd come to her senses and come back to you and to me. Next thing I knew—" Hargett shook his head, recalling "—I had divorce papers in my hand. And sole custody of you."

Some of the old hurt and confusion came back to hit Brady, full blast. "If she had loved us, she wouldn't have left us, Dad," Brady said bitterly. If she hadn't left, she might not have moved to

California and died in that multicar pileup on the interstate when Brady was five.

"And maybe your mother was just scared," Hargett countered in a calm, compassionate way that let Brady know his father had at last put the past to rest the way it should have been retired, years ago. "Maybe if your mother and I had just tried, we could have worked things out," Hargett said evenly. "The point is, I used my battalion of lawyers and made it impossible for her to come back. I boxed her in, the same way I boxed you in with the terms of the trust. And she died, thinking what I wanted her to think, that you and I were much better off without her, than with her. When it simply wasn't true."

Brady swallowed. "You're saying she might have wanted to come back to us?"

Hargett shrugged. "I'm saying I don't know. I never gave us a chance to find that out. And now it's too late. We can't go back and fix things with her, or give you the mother you should have had all those years. But there are business and financial matters that can be put to rights and that's why I came to see you this morning. I wanted to talk to you about that deal we made when you left nearly two years ago."

Brady looked his father straight in the eye. As long as they were speaking what was in their hearts, he figured he had to tell his dad this, too. "I don't care about my inheritance, Dad. I never have. All I've ever wanted was to be my own man, same as you."

"And you've done that," Hargett replied, with no small amount of pride in his voice. "Which is what I came to tell you this morning. I talked to my lawyers. I'm giving you your inheritance, free and clear. No more terms, no more restrictions. It's yours to do with what you wish."

Brady studied his father. This was a big change, one that had been long in coming. It also meant he had finally proved himself to his father. "No more pressure to come back to work for Anderson Oil?" he asked.

Hargett shook his head as he clamped an affectionate hand on Brady's shoulder. His eyes were serious. "I've put the idea of the two of us working side by side away. I realize now you don't have the passion for it that I do, and it takes real passion to run a company or build up a ranch. I want you to follow your dreams, son. I want you to follow your heart."

"I want to thank you," Patricia Weatherby said when she caught up with Kelsey at the ranch late that afternoon. She cast a curious glance at the stack of Brady's shirts draped over a porch chair.

"I talked to Rafe Marshall a little while ago. He explained everything and we're going to try it again tomorrow night."

Kelsey moved a stack of Brady's blue jeans so Patricia could sit down. "Are you going back to the Gilded Lily?" she asked.

"No, we figure that place is jinxed as far as the two of us are concerned. We want to do something more our style, so we're going to go to the Armadillo and have chili dogs and sodas and play putt-putt golf. I think it'll be a lot of fun and so does Rafe. He is such a nice man, Kelsey."

"I've always thought so." Kelsey moved a box of Brady's belongings off a chair and sat down, too. She looked at Patricia seriously. "I'm glad you're giving him another chance."

The corners of Patricia's lips curved up ruefully. "I almost didn't, you know. My experience with Cal, Molly's father, left me pretty gun-shy when it came to men."

Kelsey nodded and sighed. She knew that feeling. Given what she had just been through with Brady, the way he had turned her heart upside down and then stomped on it, she didn't think she'd ever love again. Not after the way he had heartlessly used her, all so he could collect his inheritance. Not that she wouldn't have helped him had he been straight with her. She would have. It was the fact that he hadn't trusted her enough to tell her the truth, about the trust or his father, that really stuck in her craw.

Patricia continued sadly, shaking her head, "I was such a fool, Kelsey."

"Been there and done that, too," Kelsey said. She couldn't believe the way she had opened herself up to Brady, only to have it all thrown right back in her face.

"Cal kept promising me he would get a divorce and marry me."

"But then didn't," Kelsey said, recounting what she already knew.

Patricia nodded grimly. "He said his wife wouldn't give him a divorce, and he couldn't leave his other kids. He had five back in Louisiana. So I just let it go. I was just so desperate to give Molly the father she wanted and needed, that I let Cal talk me into believing we could have a family life in Houston without really being married or him actually getting divorced. He traveled back and forth between the places all the time, anyway, for work. I convinced myself the legalities didn't matter as long as Molly was happy and had a father to love her. When he died, without having made provisions for us, I was devastated."

"Why didn't you fight to keep the house you

were living in, and the car Cal had leased for you?" Kelsey asked curiously.

Patricia frowned. "I thought about it, but I knew it would involve years of legal wrangling, a lot of money for lawyers. Plus, Cal's family was very powerful and well-connected. They had threatened to drag both Molly and me through the mud if we contested the will and made a claim on Cal's estate, and I didn't want Molly to have to go through that. So instead I decided to start over and make a new life for us and we ended up here."

Kelsey knew Patricia wasn't confiding all this to her now, just for the heck of it. "You're trying to tell me something, aren't you?" Kelsey guessed after a moment.

Patricia nodded. "I loved a man who was so wealthy, who had such a sense of his own entitlement, he didn't care who he hurt or who he lied to as long as he made sure all of his needs were met. Brady's not like that."

Kelsey sighed. She studied the look on Patricia's face. "You heard he's an Anderson Oil Company heir, didn't you?"

"Yeah. Everyone in town has. He's been telling people himself, and walking around introducing Hargett Anderson as his dad."

Kelsey paused to digest that bit of news. "That's good. I'm glad they've worked out whatever the difficulty between them was." She wanted Brady to be close to his father.

"Which leaves only one problem," Patricia said as Dani drove up, parked her car and got out. "The difficulty between you and Brady, whatever that is."

"My thought exactly," Dani Chamberlain said, coming up on the porch to join them. "I heard the news about who Brady is, and wondered how you were taking the news." Dani looked at the belongings stacked on the front porch. "Guess this answers my question."

Kelsey cleared a place beside her, so the pregnant Dani could sit down. "You know how fickle I am," Kelsey said, doing her best to make light of the situation.

"You stopped being fickle the day you hooked up with Brady," Dani argued.

Kelsey lifted a brow.

"Think about it," Dani continued. "You said you wanted to be a rancher last summer. You did that. You've overcome tremendous odds and a lot of family dissension to make this place a success and you've done that. And through it all, Brady has been by your side, first as your friend and the person who shared your same dreams, then as your partner, and finally as your husband."

"He only married me and went into partnership

with me because he wanted to get his inheritance. And he had to own a ranch, and make a success of it, to do that."

"Hogwash," Dani said. "He could have gotten Wade McCabe, or even Travis McCabe, to help him there. He went into partnership with you because he wanted to be with you, period. I'm not saying he didn't make mistakes along the way. From what I've been able to see, you both did that. But he never stopped loving you or caring about you, and he still does, otherwise he wouldn't be driving up the lane now."

Kelsey's heart skipped a beat as she followed Dani's gaze. Sure enough, Brady was driving up the lane in his pickup truck. And he wasn't wasting any time about it, either.

Abruptly, she wished she had never taken all of Brady's belongings and carried them down to the porch. But she had, and it was too late to rectify it.

Her heart in her throat, she watched as he parked his truck so it wasn't blocking anyone else's vehicle, and climbed out. His eyes locked with hers, he kept right on coming, not stopping until he was just in front of her. He tipped his hat at Patricia and Dani. "Ladies, good to see you, but I need to talk to my wife."

Patricia and Dani nodded. Both looked at Brady and Kelsey as if wishing them luck on working things out, then headed off to their respective vehicles. Kelsey waited until they had both driven away, before she said, "Uh, about your stuff—"

He eyed her thoughtfully. "Looks like you have been doing some rearranging."

Wasn't that the understatement of the year, considering everything he had left in the house was now sitting on the front porch, while everything she owned was still inside. "A little," Kelsey confirmed. "But I'm not finished yet." If things went the way she hoped, she'd be putting it all back, pronto.

"I would hope not," Brady said, in the same crisp, matter-of-fact tone he always used when they talked about ranch business. "But we'll get to that in a minute. Right now I've got something more important to say." He paused and looked her straight in the eye. "I was wrong not to tell you about the terms of my inheritance, Kelse. And I swear on everything that's good and right in this world that I will never do anything like that again, because there's no room in any true partnership for secrets. In addition—"

Kelsey studied the documents he handed her. "You paid off the mortgage to the ranch?" That, she hadn't expected.

Brady nodded, and continued gruffly, "As well as what we owed Wade McCabe. My father gave me the money he had set aside for me, free and clear."

Kelsey swallowed. She wasn't sure if he was trying to make up with her, or break up. She only knew that the financial reasons that had existed for Brady to be with her no longer were in play. Knowing whatever happened, whatever he said, she wasn't letting him go without a fight, and a victory, Kelsey said cautiously, "Obviously, you have a plan here—"

"Don't I always?" Brady shot her a rueful, side-long grin as he sat down beside her. He took her hand in his and let both rest on his thigh. "I may as well tell you straight out," he continued with a seriousness that made her heart turn somersaults in her chest. "I think we made a mistake, Kelse, getting married the way we did, pretending to everyone else it was a love match so we could get the money, while we were telling ourselves it was a strictly business arrangement. I've come to the conclusion that circumventing the truth or doing anything in halfway measures is never a good idea, no matter what the reason."

"I have to agree with you there. We should have been honest with each other from the get-go. 'Cause if I had been…" Kelsey said, taking a deep breath and getting to her feet. Brady stood, too. She grasped his hands in hers before continuing determinedly, "I would have told you that I've been in love with you, almost from the first day we met. I just didn't want to admit it to myself."

Brady's midnight-blue eyes took on an even darker hue as he swept her into his arms. "But you're ready to admit it now?"

"With all my heart," Kelsey confirmed, wreathing her arms around him. Going up on tiptoe, she clung to him tightly, and Brady lowered his head and delivered a long, soul-searching kiss that left them both breathless and shaking.

"Well, that's good, darling," Brady said when the languorous caress finally came to a halt, "because I'm head over heels in love with you, too." He tenderly cupped her face in his hands. "Which brings me to what I came here to say," he whispered with all the romance and the love she had ever wanted. "I think we ought to do more than just stay married, Kelse," he told her hoarsely. "I think we ought to get married all over again. Only this time," he continued firmly, "we're going to do it right. In front of all our family and friends."

"Kelsey, will you please stand still?" Jenna demanded as she put the finishing touches on Kelsey's wedding gown. "You're going to be walking down the aisle in five minutes and you've still got two buttons undone."

"Not to mention the fact we haven't given her something old, something borrowed, something blue or something new," Meg continued as six-year-old Alexandra smiled shyly and presented her aunt Kelsey with an antique gold heart to wear around her neck.

"And here is something borrowed—" Meg gave Kelsey the white handkerchief she had tucked into her sleeve on the day she married Luke.

Dani handed Kelsey a satin garter. "Something blue—"

"And the something new," Jenna said, kneeling and helping Kelsey slip on a pair of brand new white leather cowgirl boots, made especially for that day.

"Looks like I'm all set." Kelsey beamed at her three sisters and her niece. Outside, in the chapel, the organ began the strains of the wedding march. It was time.

"Nervous?" Jenna asked.

Kelsey shook her head. "With Brady out there, waiting for me? Not one bit." She knew she could handle anything as long as the two of them were together.

Hugs and kisses were exchanged all around, and then Alexandra picked up her basket and proceeded out into the vestibule and into the church, strewing flowers all along the way. The pregnant

Dani was next, followed by Jenna, and then Meg. Finally, it was Kelsey's turn. John McCabe held out his arm and walked her down the aisle.

Kelsey's heart and eyes were brimming as John officially gave her away, in her father's stead, and Brady took her hand in his. Together, they turned to face the minister and spoke what was in their hearts. "I, Kelsey, take thee, Brady, to have and to hold from this day forward...."

"For better for worse, for richer for poorer, in sickness and in health, to love and to cherish, till death do us part," Brady said, fitting the ring on her finger.

When the minister pronounced them man and wife, and Brady took her in his arms and kissed her, the whole church erupted in soft oohs and aahs, then rambunctious applause. And the celebrating continued well into the night, at the reception John and Lilah gave them at the McCabe ranch.

"Well, you did it," Meg Lockhart told John and Lilah admiringly as the guests kicked up their heels. "You helped all four of your sons find the ultimate happiness with the loves of their lives, and now all four of us Lockhart women, and your nephew Sam McCabe, have made the leap into matrimony, too."

John and Lilah looked over at Sam McCabe and

Kate Marten, who were busy enjoying the reception with their five sons, too.

"I wasn't sure we were going to be able to manage it," Lilah McCabe admitted with a relieved smile.

"But we did," John announced happily as he wrapped his arm around his wife's waist and tenderly kissed her cheek. "And now they're all settling down, right here in Laramie, and building families of their own."

"And we're happier than we've ever been," Meg added honestly as she looked at John and Lilah, who were still beaming proudly as any parents over their accomplishment. Gratitude filled her heart, as she looked at them soberly. She knew she was speaking for all of them as she continued, "I don't think any of us realize how much we had missed being near each other, until we moved back here, and were together again. But as good as that was, being close to family and old friends, in the community where we grew up, there was still something missing—for all of us."

"And that was the kind of love you only get from the person you're destined to marry," Lilah guessed.

Meg nodded. "Thanks for being there, to guide us through the rough spots," she said.

"Our pleasure." John grinned and gave Meg a hug.

"And for the record," Lilah added, leaning over to kiss and hug Meg, too, "we'll continue to be here for all of you girls, whenever, however you need us. Because that's what family is for."

On the dance floor that had been erected on the lawn, Brady tugged Kelsey even closer, luxuriating in the feeling of holding his new bride in his arms on the beautiful Indian summer night. "Have I told you how beautiful you look tonight?" he murmured, the soft surrender of her body against his like a balm to his soul.

Kelsey blushed, looking even prettier in her white satin gown, with her cinnamon-red hair swept up on top of her head. "Only about a thousand times," she admitted.

And the way she looked at him then, with a combination of lust and love and tenderness, had him feeling like the luckiest man alive. "Have I told you how much I love you?" he asked, even softer.

Kelsey nodded, her emerald-green eyes darkening seriously. "I love you, too, cowboy," she whispered throatily, "so very much."

Brady tightened his hold on her possessively, knowing she was making all his dreams come true. "Our lives are just starting now. And as good as things are," and they were incredibly good, Brady amended silently, "they're only going to get better."

Kelsey nodded her agreement as she rose on tiptoe and kissed him, with all the passion in her heart. "I can't wait."

* * * * *

FAMOUS FAMILIES

YES! Please send me the *Famous Families* collection featuring the Fortunes, the Bravos, the McCabes and the Cavanaughs. This collection will begin with 3 FREE BOOKS and 2 FREE GIFTS in my very first shipment—and more valuable free gifts will follow! My books will arrive in 8 monthly shipments until I have the entire 51-book *Famous Families* collection. I will receive 2-3 free books in each shipment and I will pay just $4.49 U.S./$5.39 CDN for each of the other 4 books in each shipment, plus $2.99 for shipping and handling.* If I decide to keep the entire collection, I'll only have paid for 32 books because 19 books are free. I understand that accepting the 3 free books and gifts places me under no obligation to buy anything. I can always return a shipment and cancel at any time. My free books and gifts are mine to keep no matter what I decide.

268 HCN 9971   468 HCN 9971

Name	(PLEASE PRINT)	
Address		Apt. #
City	State/Prov.	Zip/Postal Code

Signature (if under 18, a parent or guardian must sign)

Mail to the **Reader Service:**

IN U.S.A.: P.O. Box 1867, Buffalo, NY 14240-1867
IN CANADA: P.O. Box 609, Fort Erie, Ontario L2A 5X3

* Terms and prices subject to change without notice. Prices do not include applicable taxes. Sales tax applicable in N.Y. Canadian residents will be charged applicable taxes. This offer is limited to one order per household. All orders subject to approval. Credit or debit balances in a customer's account(s) may be offset by any other outstanding balance owed by or to the customer. Please allow 4 to 6 weeks for delivery. Offer available while quantities last. Offer not available to Quebec residents.

Your Privacy- The Reader Service is committed to protecting your privacy. Our Privacy Policy is available online at www.ReaderService.com or upon request from the Reader Service.
We make a portion of our mailing list available to reputable third parties that offer products we believe may interest you. If you prefer that we not exchange your name with third parties, or if you wish to clarify or modify your communication preferences, please visit us at www.ReaderService.com/consumerschoice or write to us at Reader Service Preference Service, P.O. Box 9062, Buffalo, NY 14269. Include your complete name and address.

FFBPA11